THE HARDY BOYS

CASEFILES

NO. 64

OPERATION
PHOENIX
NO. 1

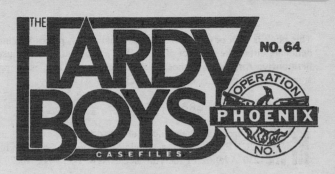

ENDANGERED
SPECIES

FRANKLIN W. DIXON

AN ARCHWAY PAPERBACK
Published by POCKET BOOKS
New York   London   Toronto   Sydney   Tokyo   Singapore

AN ARCHWAY PAPERBACK *Original*

An Archway Paperback published by
POCKET BOOKS, a division of Simon & Schuster Inc.
1230 Avenue of the Americas, New York, NY 10020

ISBN: 0-671-73100-9

First Archway Paperback printing June 1992

10 9 8 7 6 5 4 3 2 1

THE HARDY BOYS, AN ARCHWAY PAPERBACK
and colophon are registered trademarks of Simon & Schuster Inc.

THE HARDY BOYS CASEFILES is a trademark
of Simon & Schuster Inc.

Cover art by Brian Kotzky

Printed in the U.S.A.

IL6+

STAMPEDE!

Frank and Joe crouched down in the tall, dry grass. The large elephant herd was barely fifty feet away, drinking at the edge of the water hole.

As the boys watched, an enormous female elephant left the bank and walked toward Dr. Bodine, lifting her trunk and trumpeting into the air. Dr. Bodine stepped forward to greet the great beast and stroked the animal's trunk.

"Incredible," Joe said, shaking his head. "That elephant walked up to Doc Bodine like they were old friends."

Frank nodded vaguely, then sniffed the air. "You smell smoke?" He turned around. Not far from where Dr. Bodine stood, thick clouds of black smoke rose above bright red flames. The grass was ablaze.

"Fire!" Frank yelled. "And it's moving this way!"

"That's not the only thing," Joe said, pointing toward the water hole. The elephants were panicking. Twenty-ton animals were moving toward them, running faster and faster to escape the smoke and flames.

"The herd is stampeding," Joe shouted. "And we're right in their path!"

Books in THE HARDY BOYS CASEFILES® Series

Chapter

1

"TELL ME WHAT you two know about animal smuggling?" Representative Kevin Alladyce demanded in a gruff voice.

Eighteen-year-old Frank Hardy looked at Alladyce, the senior congressman from Maryland, who sat at the head of the conference table. He had chestnut-colored skin and short black hair, with distinguished tufts of gray at each temple.

Frank knew that Alladyce had dedicated his political career to working on animal conservation issues, and he was credited with passing laws that had saved several animal species from extinction. As a result, he was one of the most respected politicians in America.

"Well, I know there's an illegal market for alligator and leopard skins." Frank's younger brother, Joe, spoke up. Joe was still wondering why his father had asked him and Frank to meet him at the U.S. Customs Service office in the World Trade Center in Manhattan. Fenton Hardy sat to the right of his two sons.

Opposite the Hardys, on the other side of the table, was the assistant commissioner of the Customs Service, Ethan Daly. Daly was a heavyset man with a high forehead, deep-set blue eyes, and thinning salt-and-pepper hair. Ever since Frank and Joe had stepped into the conference room, the commissioner had studiously ignored them and barely nodded to their father. He was ill at ease, and Frank had a feeling the meeting annoyed him.

"Ivory, too," Frank added, remembering a newscast he had seen recently. "Elephants are being killed for their tusks."

Alladyce nodded sadly. "Worldwide, there's a five-billion-dollar-a-year market for the stuff."

Joe gave a low whistle and ran a hand through his blond hair. "What do the smugglers do? Shoot everything that moves?"

"Just about." Alladyce aimed a remote control at a VCR and TV monitor at the far end of the room. "One of our custom agents in Kenya managed to track some poachers and secretly made this video tape in Kenya while concealed in the underbrush."

The TV screen showed a broad grassy plain, with a thick forest on one side. An enormous

2

elephant with long, curved white tusks burst from the forest in a panicked state. Half a dozen men dressed in khaki camouflage suits emerged from the undergrowth behind it.

Suddenly the men raised powerful rifles and began to fire. Frank grimaced when he saw blood explode along the great beast's gray skin. The bull elephant lumbered to a stop, struggling desperately to stay on its feet. Finally, with crimson blood streaming from its side, it crumpled to its knees and tumbled over. The dying elephant raised its head once, bellowed in anger and agony, fell back, and was still.

Immediately the hunters ran toward the carcass. One of them carried a gasoline-powered chainsaw. Moving quickly and efficiently, he sawed off one of the elephant's great ivory tusks. He started on the second one while two men strained to hoist the heavy first tusk over their shoulders. Soon, with the second tusk free, the poachers disappeared into the bush.

Congressman Alladyce stopped the tape. There was only stunned silence in the conference room. Joe glanced at Frank and recognized the anger in his older brother's brown eyes. The savage killing had affected both of them the same way.

Congressman Alladyce spoke first. "By the end of this century the African elephant could be extinct because of the illegal market for ivory," he said grimly, shaking his head with sadness. He looked over at Assistant Commissioner Ethan Daly. "Brief the Hardys on what's happened since we received this videotape."

Daly sighed and nervously tapped his fingers on the polished table. Once again it seemed to Frank that the public servant wasn't happy about their being there.

"That footage was shot in east Africa by one of our agents only a few weeks ago," he finally said. "Before he disappeared."

Before Frank and Joe could respond, Daly leaned forward in his seat and spoke sharply to Alladyce. "And I still don't think we should go outside the department for this investigation!"

Congressman Alladyce's brows furrowed with anger. "The agent who disappeared happens to be one of my best friends," he reminded Daly in a cold voice. He added pointedly, "And so far, your people have come up with no leads."

Alladyce turned to Frank and Joe. "I asked your father if he could work on this case and locate our man. He agreed and suggested roles for you two." He turned his attention back to Daly. "I want them briefed," he said in a steely voice. "In full!"

Reluctantly Daly filled them in. "For the past year this agency has been at war with a clever ring of smugglers bringing contraband ivory, leopard skins, and exotic live animals into the country through New York."

He paused and glanced at the Hardy brothers.

4

"Two months ago Agent Christopher Lincoln tracked a shipment of ivory back to Kenya in east Africa. Lincoln and another customs agent, Martin Jellicoe, began checking out leads in Nairobi and Mombasa, a port city on the Indian Ocean. Lincoln tracked the poachers into the bush and stumbled onto some of their activities."

Alladyce gestured toward the television. "That was where the video came from. Then Chris disappeared."

"Did anyone know Chris Lincoln worked for U.S. Customs?" Joe asked.

"Lincoln was posing as a photojournalist," Daly explained. "Local authorities asked questions but came up empty."

"In other words, they're telling us that Chris disappeared into thin air," Alladyce said.

Fenton turned to Frank and Joe. "Agent Lincoln reported several leads in Mombasa. He also suspected a place called the Bodine Animal Research Compound might be involved."

"It's a wild-animal hospital run by a Dr. Rosalyn Bodine," explained Daly. "She's renowned among conservationists around the world for her success in treating injured and sick animals. Zoos and nature reserves in Europe and America ship animals to her compound for health care and research because she's the best."

Fenton nodded and turned to his sons. "I want you to look around the Animal Research

Compound while I check out the leads in Mombasa.''

Joe jabbed Frank on the shoulder. "Back to Africa," he said, obviously delighted at another opportunity to visit the exotic continent.

Frank nodded. "For a working visit," he pointed out in a serious tone. "I want to find Lincoln and help track down these poachers. It's about time someone put a stop to this cruelty."

Joe nodded. "I'm with you on that," he said firmly. "So the sooner we get over there, the better."

Frank turned to his father. "Won't we have some problems trying to keep a low profile? We don't exactly look like we're native to Africa."

Fenton shook his head. "Dr. Bodine accepts paying guests to work at the compound as a way of raising money for her operation. We've arranged a stay for you there. That'll be your cover."

"People *pay* to work!" Joe exclaimed.

Fenton Hardy smiled and nodded. "That's how famous Dr. Bodine is."

"But not beyond suspicion," Daly muttered sharply.

"I'm ready!" Joe said eagerly. "When do we go?"

Frank nodded enthusiastically. "If Lincoln's out there, we'll find him."

"That's exactly the kind of gung-ho attitude

that'll blow this cover wide open!'' Daly announced, throwing his arms into the air.

"I've already heard your objections," Alladyce told the assistant commissioner sharply. "But we want Chris Lincoln found"—he gestured at Frank and Joe—"and they're going to help us."

"Fine," Daly said in a resigned tone. He eyed the boys coldly. "We've agreed that you'll report to Agent Jellicoe while you're there."

"We report to our father," Frank objected.

Fenton Hardy put up his hand before anyone could speak. He looked at his sons. "While I'm in Mombasa, I'll be undercover and difficult to contact. I'll get in touch with you from time to time, but other than that you're responsible to Agent Jellicoe. Is that clear?"

From the corner of his eye Frank saw Daly smirking. The two brothers nodded.

"We have a doctor waiting to give you the necessary shots and malaria pills," Alladyce concluded, rising from the conference table. The meeting was over.

Frank waited while the congressman filed out with his father and Joe. Daly held the door and motioned Frank to go through.

"You know what happens to people in the wild, don't you Frank?" the public servant said when the young man stepped forward.

"What's that?" Frank asked, pausing.

7

Daly grinned, but his eyes were cold.

"Hunters who aren't careful sometimes end up being hunted."

With those words, Daly passed quickly in front of him and hurried to join the others down the hall.

Chapter
2

DURING THE WEEK that followed, Joe could hardly contain himself. Using audiotapes, he learned some basic words of Swahili. Although many languages were spoken in Kenya, including English in the cities, Swahili was the official language of the country. Frank read up on the problem of animal poaching and studied the area of east Africa.

Finally the boys' flight left New York City. Their father had left earlier. Twelve hours later the airplane touched down at Jomo Kenyatta Airport in Nairobi, Kenya. It was well past midnight.

Their father and Assistant Commissioner Daly had arranged for Martin Jellicoe to meet them. No sooner had they cleared customs than a stocky man with sunburned skin in need of a shave blocked their progress. His hair was black but flecked with gray.

"So there you are!" he boomed, an unlit cigarette bobbing from the right corner of his mouth. "Glad to see you boys made it here safe and sound. I'm Martin Jellicoe." He extended his arm to shake hands. "How was your flight?"

"Fine." Joe grinned. "Great food, bad movie."

Jellicoe lit his cigarette, blew out a mouthful of smoke, and looked the two brothers up and down. He lowered his voice and glanced around to make sure that no one was within listening distance. "The agency must be recruiting at junior proms these days."

Frank and Joe were taken aback.

"Actually," Joe said, deadpan, "we gave up our paper route for this."

"Look, boys, you can't expect me to take you too seriously." Jellicoe threw away his cigarette after only a few puffs. He led them to a jeep in the airport parking lot. The Hardys threw their duffel bags in the back and climbed in.

"I'm taking you to your hotel," Jellicoe told them. "You can sleep the rest of the night, and I'll see you in the morning. Someone will take you to the Bodine Animal Research Compound in the afternoon. It's about three and a half hours away, right in the middle of an area of heavy poaching."

As their jeep moved toward downtown Nairobi, pillbox apartment complexes and roadside merchants' booths gave way to stately Victorian homes and enormous trees whose branches bowed under the weight of thick green leaves.

The African night was calm, the air cooler than Frank expected. Nairobi's downtown looked just like an average American city, with big glass buildings and broad boulevards. But he and Joe would have to save their sightseeing for later.

Jellicoe pulled the jeep up in front of the Norwood Hotel. According to a guidebook Frank had read, the grand old building was one of the oldest in the city. Tired from the long flight, Frank and Joe took the elevator to their room on the fifth floor and quickly tumbled into bed.

The next morning Frank woke to find Joe already gone. He stuck his head out the fifth-story window. Outside, it was hot and humid. The sun was a shimmering white ball in a hazy sky. Quickly he dressed and went down to the Norwood's dining room. The walls were made of stucco and stone, and tall posts of black wood supported a shingled awning.

Just as Frank expected, Joe was sitting at a table, digging into a plate piled high with scrambled eggs, bacon, sliced pineapple, and freshly baked muffins. Frank stopped by the buffet table and filled a plate before joining his brother.

Joe chuckled when his brother sat down. "My second helping."

"I haven't eaten since dinner on the plane, yesterday," Frank said. He'd barely started in on his breakfast when the brothers heard Martin Jellicoe's boisterous voice.

"If you've finished eating, we have to get going, boys." The customs agent was striding through the dining room toward their table.

Joe had annoyance written across his face in billboard-size letters. "For some reason I like this guy less and less," he hissed.

"Be cool," Frank said to try to calm his hot-headed brother. "We have to work with this guy."

He turned toward Jellicoe, who was pulling a chair up to the table.

"Think we can get a little tour of Nairobi before we go out to the Bodine compound?" Frank asked.

Jellicoe shrugged. "If that's what you want. Or I can take you out to a place called the Nairobi Animal Habitat. It's a zoo. Give you a first look at some big-game animals."

Frank checked with Joe and the younger Hardy nodded.

"Sure thing," Frank said.

An hour later the Hardys and Jellicoe were strolling through the entrance to what looked to Joe like a large children's zoo. Acres of open grass and trees allowed young animals to roam freely. There were also corrals where people could touch some of the less dangerous beasts. One contained three young giraffes. A wooden terrace had been constructed around the side that faced the giraffes. Eight feet high and several feet long, it afforded a good view of the grounds. Visitors could actually feed the giraffes.

After climbing the platform, Joe eagerly grabbed some of the special grain provided and allowed a giraffe to nibble from his hand.

Frank spoke to Jellicoe. "Assistant Commissioner Daly told us that before he disappeared, Lincoln suspected that the Bodine Animal Research Compound might be involved in the poaching somehow," he said.

Jellicoe nodded. "Once Lincoln and I narrowed down our list of suspects, the folks at the Bodine compound—including the famous Dr. Bodine herself—were high on that list."

A giraffe sniffed at Jellicoe's chest. He grimaced and moved away.

"What's Dr. Bodine like?" Frank asked. Before Jellicoe answered, Frank noticed a redheaded man wearing dark glasses stop behind them a few feet back. Something about the way the stranger lingered within hearing distance made Frank feel edgy.

"Dr. Rosalyn Bodine." Jellicoe pronounced her name with mock authority and a fake British accent. "Born in Kenya. Father American, mother a *Kiwi*."

Joe turned away from feeding the giraffe and gave Jellicoe a puzzled look. "Kiwi?" he asked.

"A citizen of New Zealand, boys," Jellicoe explained. "Her parents were wildlife nuts, so she followed in their footsteps. Studied in the U.S., Europe, and some of the Asian countries." His eyes narrowed. "All the places you need contacts to succeed in smuggling animals."

"But she's highly respected in her field," Frank pointed out. "Why would she throw away her career by getting involved in something as terrible as animal poaching?"

"Money!" Jellicoe said with great certainty. "According to Lincoln, Dr. Bodine's parents left her with enough to start the research facility, but that's all gone now. That's why she started taking on paying guests like yourself, just to keep the place going. But still she doesn't pay all the bills. So Lincoln and I figured she saw an easy way to make a few extra bucks on the side and keep her operation going."

"Does she run her place by herself or is there a number-two person at the compound?" Joe asked.

"African fellow by the name of Oyamo," Jellicoe answered. "He's foreman and in charge of day-to-day things—feeding, tracking, and such. But most of the people there are animal lovers who pay to work, like you two are supposed to be." Jellicoe shook his head. "Anyone who pays to work somewhere has got to be a flunky."

While he listened to Jellicoe ramble on, Frank noticed that the redheaded man he'd spotted earlier was still in the same spot.

"Did you and Agent Lincoln have any hard proof against Dr. Bodine?" Joe asked.

"Whatever we had we sent back to Daly at headquarters," Jellicoe replied. He lit a cigarette. "Chris came across the poachers twice in the bush. The second time he trailed them—right back to Bodine's compound. He lost them before he could get a positive ID. He told me he was driving out to the compound to look around some more. He never came back."

"That's it?" Frank asked.

"Look, boys," Jellicoe said. "There are thousands of square miles of land out there and one man who's probably already dead. Daly tells me he's sending me some help, and what do I get? Junior G-men in designer sneakers."

Frank took a deep breath. "We're experienced investigators," he said patiently.

Jellicoe snorted. "Your father is an experienced investigator."

"And that's who we're here to help," Joe said firmly.

Jellicoe looked skeptically at the blond young man. "Well, he hasn't contacted me yet. Until he does, I'm in charge and you report to me."

"How do we get in touch with you if we learn anything?" Frank asked.

Jellicoe snorted again. "Don't worry—I'll be

keeping my eye on you." The customs agent flashed Frank and Joe a mocking smile. "When you least expect it."

A friendly giraffe approached and sniffed at Jellicoe's hand. He pushed it away roughly.

"I've had enough of these animals," he said, tossing his partly smoked cigarette down and grinding it out with his foot. He wiped his brow and glanced up at the hot yellow sun. "I'll meet you two back at the jeep." The agent waved goodbye and took off.

"If I never see that clown again"—Joe sputtered when Jellicoe was out of sight—"it'll be too soon."

"He is kind of a jerk," Frank agreed. "Let's chill out while we look around a little more."

The Hardys strolled the grounds, fascinated by the numbers of gazelles and antelope bounding across the fields behind earthen wall enclosures.

Suddenly Frank whispered to Joe. "We've got company. We're being tailed."

"Where?" Joe asked casually, not showing any sign of the danger he sensed.

"About twenty feet behind us," Frank muttered.

Pretending to peer at some nearby zebras, Joe searched the path behind them. "A redheaded guy in dark glasses?" he asked.

Frank nodded. "Let's find a quiet place where we can have a talk with our new friend." He pointed to a roped-off area of dense trees. The

brothers vaulted the rope and crouched behind some shrubs.

"We'll jump him when he passes," Frank whispered.

"How long do you think we'll have to wait?" Joe asked in a low voice. Suddenly he felt the hard barrel of a gun jab into his spine.

"Not very long," a voice growled behind them. "Not long at all."

Chapter

3

"TURN AROUND nice and easy," the man ordered.

Frank and Joe turned slowly.

The redheaded man was still wearing his dark glasses. A camera was slung over one shoulder, and Frank followed the strap down to the man's hands. It was empty; only his index finger was extended to poke Joe again.

"I thought I taught you better than that."

"Dad!" Joe exclaimed. "Why are you dressed like that?"

"And when did you get here?" Frank asked.

Fenton Hardy removed his dark glasses. His eyes were deep brown instead of blue.

Joe was stunned. "Contact lenses! You've really gone all the way with this disguise."

"I'm pretending to be a big-time buyer of live exotic animals, leopard skins, and ivory. This morning I got a call from someone who may have something to sell. I'm supposed to meet with him tomorrow in Mombasa."

Frank told Joe, "Mombasa is a beach resort town on the Indian Ocean."

Joe threw his hands up in the air. "Oh, that's just great. Dad winds up with girls at a beach while we chase chimps."

"Don't take your assignment lightly," Fenton warned. "Remember, the last time Chris Lincoln was seen, he was heading for the Bodine compound."

"Do you think he's dead?" Frank asked.

Fenton shook his head. "He may have gone deeper undercover with the poachers. Or he may be their prisoner. Any way you look at it, there is danger. Keep your eyes and ears open."

"We'll be careful," Frank promised.

Fenton handed him a slip of paper with a phone number on it. "You can contact me through this number in Mombasa. They're people I trust."

Frank frowned. "Are you going to check in with Jellicoe?"

"Not yet. First I want to try to establish a link with the poachers." Fenton Hardy put his dark sunglasses back on and was once again the red-haired stranger. "I have a feeling this case is going to be hard." Fenton Hardy turned and walked up the path.

Frank and Joe left the bushes and found Jellicoe waiting in the parking lot, smoking a cigarette in the driver's seat of his jeep.

He drove them back to Nairobi and dropped them off at their hotel. Frank and Joe barely had time to shower and grab a quick lunch. At one o'clock they were waiting in the front lobby of the Norwood when a white van drove up. Bodine Animal Research Compound was stenciled on the side door. A young African man got out and moved lightly up the steps toward them.

"Jambo!" the young man said. "You are Frank and Joseph Hardy?"

"Just call me Joe, please." Joe smiled.

"I am Lucas Oyamo Nganu," he replied. "I prefer Oyamo, if you please."

"Hi, Oyamo," Joe said, extending his hand.

Oyamo led the way to the van. A young woman with coffee-colored skin opened the rear door.

"This is Keesha Imanu," Oyamo said. "She also works for Dr. Bodine."

Keesha was a slender girl with her hair styled in long, thin braids that hung to her shoulders. The braids accentuated her high cheekbones and her narrow chin. She kept looking down, as if she were extremely shy.

"Hi—uh, I mean, *jambo*." Joe smiled at her.

"Jambo, Keesha," Frank said.

Keesha smiled. *"Habari ya jioni."*

Frank looked at Joe and shrugged.

"My Swahili begins and ends with hello," Frank said with a grin.

"She said good afternoon," Joe explained.

Keesha laughed, obviously delighted that Joe had understood. "I'm sure your Swahili will improve," she told Frank.

Frank and Joe threw their packs into the back. Keesha motioned them toward the side door while Oyamo walked to the driver's seat.

Frank noticed Dr. Rosalyn Bodine the moment he stepped into the van. Her sandy blond hair was pulled back in a loose ponytail, her eyes were deep green, and her angular face had a touch of softness that made her appear to be kind.

"Good afternoon," she said. "You're punctual. That's a good start. I'm Dr. Rosalyn Bodine." She reached over the seat to shake hands with both of them. The van pulled away from the Norwood Hotel.

"Please begin familiarizing yourselves with this material," Dr. Bodine continued, handing them two thick folders. "It explains what we do at the compound. You'll be put to work immediately, so you may as well bone up on the ride. We have a three and a half hour journey ahead of us. On rough roads." With that, the famous veterinarian turned back to her own large file of notes and graphs.

Joe gestured at Frank and then toward the doctor with a silent shrug. She didn't seem to find her paying guests very interesting, Joe thought.

Frank nodded but quickly opened his folder. He began glancing through the material. He read information on baby elephants, mother's milk, and tusk size; the Bodine bird sanctuary; the studies on snake venoms and the habits of various predators.

Beside him, Joe thumbed through the material and groaned softly. This was too much like cramming for a test at school to please him. The van sped through the countryside, with an endless view of farms and fields. They could smell the different crops as they drove past—coffee, maize, and tropical fruits. Then the minivan passed through rolling hills that overlooked deep valleys. Rivers and lakes cut bright blue gashes through the reddish brown earth. Nairobi was much the same as any American city. But now Frank felt they were truly in Africa.

Joe was equally absorbed by the landscape and the people they passed walking the roadsides wrapped in colorful robes and jewelry. Sometimes, small herds of zebras and camels roamed beside the road. After a long ride Oyamo turned onto a rutted gravel road that led across a grassy plain dotted with trees and clumps of bushes. Giraffes stretched to feed on leaves, and baboons swung from branches high in the trees.

"This is really the jungle," Joe said to Frank.

His brother shook his head. "I know what you mean," he said. "But actually this is grassland and it's called the veld. A real jungle is so thick with trees and brush that you need a machete to hack your way through it."

In the front seat Dr. Bodine overheard Frank's comments. She turned around and smiled. "I see someone knows the geography of southern Africa," she said, obviously impressed.

Frank blushed. "I did a little reading," he said modestly.

Finally in the late afternoon they rolled into the Bodine Animal Research Compound. It was surrounded by a high chain-link fence with a gatekeeper at the entrance.

The van followed a long, gracious drive lined with palm trees that led to a large Victorian mansion with a screened-in front porch supported by tall white columns.

"It looks as if we're stepping onto an old plantation," Frank said to Joe.

A paved parking area stretched off to one side of the old house. Beyond it a number of simple wooden bungalows lined both sides of the drive. The road continued past these outbuildings and disappeared just beyond a copse of small trees. Frank could make out the top of a chain-link fence farther on. Rising in front of it and above it were shed roofs made of corrugated metal.

"That is where the animals are kept," Keesha explained.

Oyamo slowed the van in front of the Victorian house and dropped Dr. Bodine off. She stood by the rear door and spoke to the Hardys through the open window.

"Oyamo will take you to your quarters in the men's dormitory," she told them. "And I'll see you at dinner in the mess hall."

Oyamo pulled the van away from the porch and drove farther onto the compound. Behind the main house was a chain-link cage the size of a small building, filled with dozens of colorful birds of different species. Their singing and squawking created quite a racket. Just beyond the cage was a fenced corral.

Joe's eyes grew wide when he saw the sole inhabitant.

"One medium-size elephant." Frank laughed. As the van passed, the beast raised its long trunk and trumpeted a loud greeting.

Keesha laughed, too. "Her name is Rafiki. It means 'friend' in Swahili. You will find that she is very glad to meet new visitors."

"What are all these buildings here?" Frank asked as the van came to the first of half a dozen bungalows. Each building was faced with a row of wide windows and had a single door at each end.

"That's the mess hall," Keesha explained, pointing to the first building they passed. "Across from it is the recreation building, where you will find a television and games such as Ping-Pong for your free time in the evenings. The rest of these are bunkhouses for our guests.''

Oyamo stopped the van in front of the last bungalow, a long, one-story building that resembled an army barracks.

"Let me show you to your bunks," Oyamo said. "An hour remains before dinner, and I will give you a tour of the compound."

Oyamo opened the door so the Hardys could unload their bags from the back of the van and carry them inside. The dormitory had two long rows of neatly made army-style beds. At the foot of each bed was a box where guests could leave pieces of luggage.

"There are twelve workers in each dormitory," Keesha explained. "Everyone is busy now with their chores. You will meet them soon."

The Hardys were assigned two beds at the farthest end of the dormitory. They left their duffel bags on their beds and followed Oyamo and Keesha back outside.

On the other side of the dormitory, partly hidden by a row of thick shrubs with strange, brilliant red flowers, Joe noticed a large garage. Jeeps, trucks, and several vans were parked out front.

"That is our motor pool," Oyamo explained.

"But come this way first," Keesha said with

25

a mischievous smile. "I know Rafiki would like to meet you."

Frank and Joe strode across the hard-baked ground to the corral.

"You can pet her," Oyamo assured them. "She's very friendly."

"Glad to meet you, Rafiki," Frank said, reaching out to stroke the elephant's forehead.

"Her mother was killed by poachers two years ago," Keesha recounted. "We have been looking after her ever since."

"Sorry to hear that," Frank said. Eager to see more of the compound, he started walking away. Rafiki stretched out her trunk and wrapped it around his leg.

"I think she likes my jeans," Frank joked.

"I think she likes *you*," Joe teased.

Oyamo and Keesha led Frank and Joe down a path past the motor pool, where the road branched out in different directions. Dr. Bodine's compound was vast. There were cages of all sizes that sheltered lions, zebras, monkeys, gazelles, badgers, and even a limping jackal with a broken leg bound in a cast. Another cage held an elderly vulture that, according to Keesha, was too old to survive in the wilderness. Oyamo showed them a litter of playful leopard kittens that were only a few weeks old.

"Their mother was killed by poachers," he explained sadly. "If we had not found her lair, her kittens would have starved to death."

The last stop on the tour was a large building that housed a laboratory, with an animal hospital attached to it. There Frank and Joe met several veterinarians and lab technicians, as well as other paying guests who shared the same dormitory.

Two of them, Dean and Doug, were American college students working on their degrees. Keir was an Australian man who was spending a year traveling around the world. He had decided to stay at the compound for several months to help out. The Rutherfords, a middle-aged couple from England, told the Hardys they had dedicated their lives to saving endangered species and had come to work for Dr. Bodine during their vacation.

Everyone seemed very busy, washing down animals, administering medicine, and cleaning out cages. Frank wondered how he and Joe would find time for sleuthing when they started working as hard as these people.

"What's this?" Joe asked, pausing beside a glass tank set against one wall.

Oyamo stopped. "That is the *Bitis arietans*," he said dryly. "Most commonly known as—"

"A puff adder," Frank finished for him. "Plentiful in Kenya and extremely dangerous."

"You know about snakes?" Oyamo asked, surprised.

"I know about all kinds of animals," Frank replied. He paused a moment and decided to

27

seize the opportunity to get some information. "I saw some great animal photos in a magazine recently by a photographer named Chris Lincoln. The article said he was working in this area. Is he still around?"

Oyamo stared blankly at Frank. "Mr. Lincoln visited here a long time ago—but only briefly." Without another word the Kenyan started for the door.

"Do you know where Lincoln went?" Frank called out as he and Joe followed Oyamo outside.

"How would I know such a thing?" Oyamo asked with annoyance. He glanced at his watch. "Dinner is in ten minutes. I will see you in the mess hall." He left them without another word.

"That got you nowhere," Joe observed.

Frank was thoughtful. "I'll try again. Later. Let's wash up."

Dinner was a long, friendly affair, and they met so many other guests that Frank and Joe soon lost track of names. By the time dinner was over, they were ready for bed.

In the bunkhouse Frank stretched out on his cot, only a few feet from Joe's. Six beds lined each side of the bungalow. Three low-hanging lamps ran down the center of the room, casting round pools of soft light. Most guests lay in bed, reading quietly or writing letters. Warm, gentle breezes blew in through the screened windows.

"I can use the sleep," Frank said through a yawn. "It'll make up for last night."

Joe chuckled as he slipped under his covers. "You're getting old, big brother."

"Good night, little brother," Frank said.

Joe mumbled something and turned over. A few minutes later the lights were turned out. For a while Frank lay on his back, listening to the sounds of the other men in the bunkhouse breathing softly in their sleep. He was about to roll over when he felt a cool, smooth sensation across his left ankle.

It was as if someone were dragging a rope over his foot and up his leg. Frank froze. The movement continued onto his thigh. The sheet came up as far as his waist, and a snake emerged from under the covers, writhing across his belly. In the dim blue light that filtered in through the window from an outside lamp, he could see it clearly.

It was the puff adder. One wrong move and Frank was dead meat.

Chapter

4

FRANK CHOKED BACK a scream. Don't move, he told himself—or you'll die! He knew Joe was sleeping only a few feet away, but there was no way for him to get his brother's attention.

He felt the snake slide smoothly across his chest and over his right arm. Then it stopped and coiled back. Its eyes shone at him like shiny dark beads. He watched the forked tongue flicker from the puff adder's open mouth and retreat, disappearing between two deadly fangs.

A bead of sweat rolled slowly down Frank's forehead and fell into his eye, stinging it. He fought every urge to move as his vision blurred with tears. The snake began to slide along his neck. He felt it stop at a spot just below his ear.

Frank remained perfectly still, not even breathing. Soon he would have to. Several beds away someone grumbled in his sleep and stirred.

The snake came to life. Frank watched with horror as it rose above his chin, its head inches from his lips. He felt its tail coil away from his right hand.

The puff adder slid forward onto Frank's face, writhing along his cheek and over his eye. Its jaws and gleaming fangs filled Frank's entire field of vision. Somewhere in the dormitory the waking man began to get out of bed. Frank heard floorboards creak. He kept his eyes focused on the part of the snake's body just behind its narrow head. The snake stiffened. Frank lashed out and grabbed it, the air exploding from his lungs in a loud yell.

A few feet away Joe Hardy was jerked abruptly from his sleep. Certain the shout came from Frank, he leapt to his feet. He saw his brother on his bed, with his sheets kicked aside. Frank held his arm out and away from him. A three-foot-long snake thrashed and coiled wildly in his hand like a whip.

"Get something to put this in!" he shouted.

The lights came on. The other residents of the dormitory began to sit up in bed, blinking against the brightness and the rude awakening.

Quickly Joe found a wastebasket and grabbed it. Keir, the Australian, and Dean, one of the American students, jumped from their beds to help. Frank dropped the snake in the basket and whipped his hand away. Joe tossed a blanket over it.

"Frank?" Joe demanded, turning to his brother. "Did it—?"

"No," Frank said, heaving a sigh of relief.

"What's going on?" a voice boomed from the door at the far end of the dormitory.

Oyamo, dressed only in shorts, stood in the barracks doorway, glaring down the long row of beds. By this time everyone was out of bed, staring in amazement at the Hardys and the covered wastebasket in the middle of the aisle.

Frank pointed at the wastebasket. "Your puff adder decided to go for a stroll."

"In Frank's bunk!" Joe said angrily.

Oyamo strode forward and stopped at the basket. He shook it gently. A sharp hiss escaped like steam.

"You were lucky, Frank," Oyamo said. "People who play with snakes usually get bitten."

"Frank wasn't playing," Joe shot back angrily. "It was put in his bed."

Oyamo looked at him. "Or perhaps someone thought a puff adder would make a unique souvenir." He picked up the wastepaper basket. "Either way, I will look into this tomorrow." Oyamo turned to the other men.

"Please go back to bed, all of you," he told them. "We will investigate this further in the morning."

After Oyamo left the dormitory, the other workers uneasily turned back to their beds.

"Quite a spot of bother," Mr. Rutherford muttered, flinging the sheet over his legs.

Keir flipped his blankets and started lifting his mattress. He looked over at the Hardys. "No bloody way I'll crawl back in between these sheets without a look-see for snakies," he said in his thick Australian accent.

Frank looked at Joe. "Not a bad idea. Whoever did this had to sneak it in here and plant it ahead of time. Let's check our bunks and lockers."

Suddenly Doug, one of the American students, hopped out of bed. "Say, the Aussie's right. How do we know there aren't more puff adders around?" Gingerly he started checking. Soon Dean and Rutherford and the other men in the dormitory were out of bed for the second time, searching high and low for more snakes. Frank and Joe checked out the wall behind their beds.

"Look at this," Joe whispered to Frank. He pointed under the bed. "There's an air vent in the wall at the head of your bed."

Frank joined his brother. A five by seven hole had been cut into the wall. It led outside, where it was covered by a wire mesh.

"Let's wait until everyone's asleep and then have a look outside," Frank suggested. "If everyone starts wandering around outside trying to help us, they might trash some clues."

Joe nodded. "Good idea."

In a few minutes it was clear that no more snakes were in the dormitory, and everyone began returning to bed. After the lights went out, the Hardys waited patiently. Soon the dormitory was quiet with the even, rhythmic breathing of sleepers.

Frank got up and sat on the edge of Joe's bed, nudging his brother. "Let's check outside."

After quietly slipping on their shoes and taking flashlights from their foot lockers, they crept outside. A moment later they were kneeling by the barrack's wall. Frank's flashlight beam swept along the wooden planks to where the ventilation hole led outside.

Joe examined the mesh covering the opening closely. "This is held on by six screws," he said. Then he easily pulled it away from the wall. "Four are missing."

Frank turned his flashlight toward the ground and circled the beam carefully.

"Here they are." He picked up several tiny screws from the ground. "Someone didn't take the time to put them all back."

"And that same someone tried to kill you," Joe added, standing and facing his brother squarely.

Frank cast his gaze over the still compound. Kerosene lanterns lit a few areas near the showers and the old house, but the night was pitch black, and the darkness pressed against the thin pools of light. Most of the buildings were no more than large shadows. Strange sounds rose and fell like whispers in the dark.

"We'd better get some sleep," Frank said finally, turning back to Joe. "I have a feeling things aren't going to get easier."

After waking at dawn, Frank and Joe stood in line for showers and watched the sun rise, purple and reddish in the east. Quickly it changed to soft orange and finally to yellow. The sky was intensely blue. They grabbed breakfast in the mess hall, and then assembled in the main yard with the other paying guests to hear duty call for the day. Rosalyn Bodine was ready to address the troops.

"As you know," Dr. Bodine began, "the wildebeest migration has begun. Thousands of them will be traveling through here on their way across the Kenya-Tanzania border. Also, several elephant herds are on the move to new watering holes, and two lion prides have been spotted near the Kimana village. This means a great deal of spotting work, so I'll assign teams to observe these various events."

Rosalyn Bodine paused for a moment and brushed back a few stray strands of blond hair that fluttered against her cheek. "Speaking of elephants," she continued, "tomorrow we will reintroduce Rafiki to one of the wild herds."

Several of the guest workers erupted into a round of applause.

"Your favorite elephant," Joe muttered to Frank.

"Rafiki must be a celebrity around here," Frank nodded.

"Rafiki has been without a herd for two years, and it's time to let her return to the wild," Dr. Bodine told them. "She needs to learn how to live as an elephant, not as a human."

This time everyone in attendance applauded, including the Hardys.

"Okay, everyone, let's get to work."

As the rest of the workers went about their assignments, Dr. Bodine called Frank and Joe over. As they approached her, they could see her eyes narrowing.

"Oyamo told me about the snake last night. I don't like pranks."

"You think I removed that snake from the lab?" Frank asked in disbelief.

Dr. Bodine hesitated. "Let's just say that I'll be watching you two," she finally said.

Joe started to protest when Frank shot him a warning to keep him quiet.

Dr. Bodine glanced at some papers on a clipboard she held and glanced at Joe. "I understand you're a bit of a mechanic."

"I'm pretty good at minor repairs," the younger Hardy admitted.

Dr. Bodine nodded with satisfaction. "Maybe later today you can help out at the motor pool. This morning, however, I'm sending you out with Oyamo and a few others to spot leopards. Listen to Oyamo. Follow his lead. The bush isn't a picnic ground.''

Rosalyn stalked away toward the animal hospital.

"Looks like we're roaming the range, today,'' Joe said to Frank when they were alone.

"Too bad. I was hoping we'd get a chance to look around the compound.'' Frank glanced up at the blazing sun. "If nothing else, we'll get a great tan.''

Within an hour Frank and Joe were seated in a six-passenger jeep, tearing along a back trail with Oyamo at the wheel. Keesha sat up front with Oyamo, while another compound worker, a friendly Kenyan named Sammy, shared the rear seat with the Hardys.

The twisting, hilly road was narrow and rutted. On either side, Joe observed, thorn-covered bushes formed a dense wall. From time to time the car dipped down steep inclines that led to dry riverbeds and craggy ravines. Suddenly Oyamo turned a corner and the land opened up into a vast plain of grass on which great herds of antelope grazed.

"Look, there's a herd of zebras,'' Joe told Frank, pointing to a cluster of trees and bushes. "And over there, gazelles.''

Frank was intrigued by how the land changed so quickly. Here it was lush and green, with brick-red earth. But close by the land was barren and dry, the soil little more than fine gray dust that was blown across the plains.

At the base of a high hill Oyamo stopped the jeep. "We will check the area for leopards," he explained. "Please bring your binoculars."

Frank and Joe followed Oyamo, Keesha, and Sammy to the top of the hill.

"What a sight!" Joe exclaimed. In the distance the pale gray land had been stripped of grass, brush, and trees.

"How does anything survive out there?" Frank asked Oyamo.

"Some things do not," Oyamo replied. "The animals move from place to place, searching for water and food."

Just then Frank spotted several cows ambling slowly in the heat a hundred yards below them. Behind them walked a man draped in brightly colored cloth. He carried a long walking stick in one hand. "What about him?"

"He is a Masai," Oyamo explained. "They are a tribe that clings to the old ways, and they lead their cattle everywhere."

Sammy stepped up next to Frank. "They are also a threat to the endangered animals."

"Why?" Frank asked.

"In their tradition a young man must prove he is ready to be a warrior by single-handedly killing a lion. He must do it with only a spear, shield, and knife. The Masai are as deadly as the poachers."

"That is not true," Oyamo said, suddenly defensive. "There is a watering hole to the south where we will find leopards," he said, abruptly changing the subject. "Let us go." Angrily he started down the hill to the jeep.

Keesha joined Oyamo and they walked away in silence.

Sammy watched them go and chuckled. "I can always get him angry by talking about the Masai."

"Why does he defend them?" Joe asked.

"I've said more than enough," Sammy said quickly. He hurried down the hill after Oyamo and Keesha, leaving the Hardys to bring up the rear.

Once they were back on the road, Joe leaned forward to talk to Keesha and Oyamo in the front seat.

"Has there been any poaching around here, Keesha?" he asked.

Keesha appeared to be edgy. "A little maybe," she replied cautiously.

In the backseat Sammy had overheard and replied, "Are you kidding? Poachers have been hitting the region like crazy."

"Up ahead!" Oyamo exclaimed suddenly, hitting the jeep's brakes. The body of a large, spotted cat lay in the road.

"*Duma*," Sammy said quietly.

"That is Swahili for 'cheetah,' " Keesha explained to the Hardys.

39

Oyamo pulled up next to the body. "Stay in the jeep," he instructed. Cautiously he got out and moved toward the bush.

"He'll make sure there are no wild animals lurking about," Keesha said.

A moment later Oyamo signaled that it was clear. Everyone left the car and gathered around the dead cheetah.

Joe noticed something glinting deep in the animal's fur. He knelt by the body. "Someone with a tranquilizer gun did this." Joe pulled a small metal dart from the cheetah's neck and examined it closely. The needle hollow had contained a deadly poison, which had killed the cheetah instantly.

"The body is still warm," said Frank, "which means we must have interrupted whoever did this."

Just then they heard someone—or something—crashing through the undergrowth on the other side of the road.

"That sounds like someone running away," said Sammy. "Let's go after him."

He and Oyamo started toward the bush.

"No!" Keesha exclaimed. "Whoever it is may be armed."

"If we get a look at them, we can give a description to the rangers," Oyamo insisted. He and Sammy disappeared into the trees.

Joe's eyes flashed. "Coming, Frank?" he asked, starting into the dense foliage.

40

Frank looked at Keesha.

"I'll call the compound on our radio," she said. "Maybe they can send help."

"All right!" Frank followed Joe into the bush. A thick web of tangled branches and vines closed in on them when they entered the forest. Occasionally a giant tree trunk broke through the canopy of leaves, letting thin shafts of sunlight penetrate to the ground.

Joe ran full out through the bush, dodging logs and fallen trees.

"They're up ahead!" Joe called out.

Frank raced to catch up with his brother, but Joe was moving like a wildman, swatting branches aside and vaulting boulders. Suddenly Frank saw the ground give way where his brother was running.

Joe felt the earth disappear beneath his feet. He plunged through a pile of leaves into a dark pit. Then he felt something lash around his head. Suddenly his fall was stopped, and with a painful jerk at his throat, he was yanked into the air.

He bounced from the end of a long rope tied to an overhead tree branch. Around his neck a noose tightened, strangling him.

His head felt as if it would explode, and his neck was ready to snap. His hands clawed at the deadly rope while his lungs screamed for air. Pinpoints of light danced before his eyes before everything went black.

Chapter

5

"JOE!" Frank cried out as his brother was yanked violently into the air. A hunter's snare with a hangman's noose and rope was attached to a tree branch high overhead. Joe suddenly stopped clawing at the rope. Frank didn't have a second to lose.

Immediately he grabbed his utility knife from his belt and pulled out the blade. Holding it firmly in his right hand, he leapt into the air and with his free hand grabbed the rope just above Joe's head. The tree branch bent under the weight of both brothers, lowering them toward the pit.

Frank swung his body, moving them back over solid ground. As their feet touched down, the rope went slack. He hacked at it savagely with the knife, severing it in a second. Joe was free.

Frank tore the noose from his brother's neck. Joe moaned. His chest jerked and rose as he took in fresh air. His eyelids fluttered and finally opened. He looked dazed and confused. He coughed before speaking in a low, raspy voice.

"I owe you one," he said with difficulty, rubbing his neck. The rope had burned a red line into the soft skin.

Frank smiled, relieved that Joe was all right. "Any time, kid brother. Any time."

Sammy and Oyamo rushed toward them through the underbrush.

"Watch out for that pit," Frank warned.

"It's a snare for catching leopards and cheetahs," Oyamo said, kneeling beside the two brothers and glancing at the severed rope.

Joe sat up. "Well, today it almost got a human."

Suddenly they all heard the roar of an engine back on the road.

"Sammy, will you stay with Joe?" Frank asked.

"Sure, but—"

Before he heard another word, Frank was racing through the bush toward the sound on the road with Oyamo close behind him. They broke into a clearing on the other side of the forest, just in time to see another jeep disappear around a bend in the road. Billowing dust made it impossible to read the license plate.

"Did you get a look at the driver?" Oyamo asked.

"No," Frank replied, panting as he caught his breath.

Just then Keesha drove up in their jeep and stopped only a few feet from Frank and Oyamo.

"I heard a car pull away and drove up to see what happened," she said. "When I got through to the compound, Dr. Bodine sounded very upset. She said she would phone the ranger and wants us to return immediately."

"Okay," Frank said. "Let's get Joe and Sammy and head back."

A short while later Oyamo drove through the gates of the Bodine Animal Research Compound and headed up the drive toward the main house. Rosalyn Bodine was on the steps, arms akimbo, her face flushed with anger.

"What did you think you were doing out there?" she demanded as the four of them hopped out of the vehicle.

Sammy studied the tips of his walking shoes. "We thought we could get a look at the poachers."

"You are *not* rangers, Sammy," the veterinarian snapped. "And, Oyamo," she said, whirling on her foreman. "You of all people should know better!"

The African's milky brown eyes returned her hard glare, but he said nothing. Then Dr. Bodine

44

focused her attention on the Hardys. She winced when she saw the nasty red marks on Joe's neck. "It seems you nearly got yourself hanged because of your foolishness."

Joe started to reply. Frank stopped him with a nudge.

"I'll say this for everyone to hear," Rosalyn Bodine said, raising her voice and speaking to all four of them. "Leave the poachers to the rangers."

As if on cue, a jeep drove into the compound and stopped in front of the house. A ranger in matching green shirt and pants stepped from the vehicle. He was a short man in his forties, Frank observed, with a chestnut complexion and a bald spot on the top of his head. He had an easygoing manner, but his eyes were keen and alert.

"*Jambo*, Doctor," he called.

"*Jambo*, Ranger Rawji," Dr. Bodine replied. "We've been waiting. These are the young people who stumbled across the poachers."

Rawji strolled over to the group.

"You know everyone, except these two," the doctor said, pointing at the Hardys. "Ranger Pope Rawji, Frank and Joe Hardy from the United States." The brothers shook hands with the ranger.

Frank, Joe, Oyamo, and the two others related the story of the dead cheetah and the trap.

"So you didn't see who was driving the jeep?" Rawji asked when they were all finished.

"No," said Frank. "Do you think it was the same person who built that snare?"

"Probably Masai," Sammy muttered. Oyamo shot him a cold, dark look, and Keesha turned her head quickly to Oyamo.

Ranger Rawji chose his words carefully. "Many tribes use snares, Sammy. It would be difficult to say it is Masai without examining the site carefully."

Just then one of the workers ran up to Keesha. She pointed at the Hardys and whispered in the doctor's ear.

"You have a telephone call," Dr. Bodine told them, irritation sounding in her voice. "A Mr. Jellicoe. You can take it on the extension in the lab. Keesha will show you where."

The Hardys followed Keesha into the big Victorian house, leaving the doctor with Ranger Rawji. The phone was on a desk in the corner of the lab. Keesha handed Frank the receiver.

"This is Frank Hardy."

"Frank, my boy"—Jellicoe's voice boomed out from the receiver—"have you and your brother settled in?"

"Sure, Mr. Jellicoe." Frank shot a glance at Joe. "Everything's fine. We've had a couple of near misses with the local animals though." Frank told Jellicoe about the snake and the cheetah.

"You're sure you two are all right?" the agent

asked. "You can always pull out, you know. It's no skin off my back."

"We're fine," Frank told him. "It's just starting to get interesting around here."

"Let me know if you change your mind," Jellicoe told him. "By the way, I haven't been able to reach your father to tell him you arrived safely."

"All I know is that he'll be in touch with us when he's ready," Frank said smoothly.

Jellicoe cleared his throat and seemed ready to say something else. He stopped instead and said goodbye.

"Thanks, Keesha," Frank said, hanging up the phone. He and Joe left the lab and walked out through the foyer of the Victorian house.

Once they were outside, Joe asked Frank about the phone call. "Dad hasn't contacted Jellicoe yet?" he said, surprised.

Frank shook his head and frowned. "No. I wonder why not?"

Joe shook his head slowly with grim purpose. "I hope he's all right."

Frank punched his younger brother lightly on the shoulder. "Sure he's all right. As I told Jellicoe, he'll be in touch when he's ready."

Just then Joe noticed several young native men walking across the grounds. They wore the same red-and-blue-print robes that he had seen draped on the man in the wild. Their jewelry consisted of red-, blue-, black-, and white-beaded necklaces and earrings, with metal arrowheads and disks hanging from them. Their hair was styled in hundreds of short braids and dyed crimson. Several of them carried bows and arrows as well as long walking sticks.

"Masai?" Joe asked.

"Could be," Frank replied. "Let's find out."

Oyamo came around the corner of a bunkhouse and the natives greeted him. Frank and Joe stopped next to Rafiki's corral to watch the encounter. When the young elephant saw Frank, she trumpeted and headed across the corral.

"Oyamo looks angry," Joe commented, keeping his eyes on the foreman and the natives. Even at a distance the Hardys could hear a flurry of words pass between Oyamo and the Masai. Oyamo waved his arms as if he wanted the young men to go away.

"Glad you guys are here," Sammy said, appearing from behind them. He had several enormous brushes with thick hard bristles tucked under his arms. "You two have to help wash Rafiki."

Joe and Frank turned toward the elephant, who stared back at them and began flapping her ears.

Sammy grinned. "She's flirting." He handed them the brushes and pointed to a nearby garden hose and faucet.

"Great," Joe said.

Frank gestured toward the Masai. "I think

48

Oyamo wants those guys to leave," said Frank. "Are they troublemakers?"

Sammy laughed softly. "Yes, they're making trouble—but only for Oyamo. They're from a nearby village, and they know him."

Rafiki reached over the corral barrier and tried to slip her trunk into Frank's pocket. The older Hardy gently pushed it away. "They're dressed differently from the man we saw this morning," said Frank.

"They are warriors," Sammy explained. "They do not tend cattle."

"I thought so." Joe nodded. "And those aren't walking sticks, are they? They're spears."

Sammy laughed. "You are very observant."

"That's some knife one of them is carrying, too," Joe said, pushing Rafiki's playful trunk away from his ear. The Masai warrior who was doing most of the talking carried a long, shiny knife with a carved black handle at his waist.

Sammy turned on the tap, lifted the hose, and began spraying the elephant with water after they joined Rafiki in her pen. "That's a traditional Masai knife," he replied. "It is used for hunting lions. He, or someone in his village, made it."

"Sammy, you said those guys know Oyamo," Frank remarked. "How well?"

"Very well," Sammy said. "Oyamo's mother is Kikuyu, from a tribe here in Kenya. She wanted him to have a worldly education, so she sent him away to school.''

"Wait a minute," said Joe. "You said his mother was Kikuyu. What about his father?''

"Masai," Sammy told them. "Oyamo is really Masai, from a Masai village, and his people will not let him forget it.''

Rafiki wrapped her trunk around Frank's arm and pulled him toward her.

"Must be your cologne," Joe teased.

At that moment Oyamo began leading the warriors toward the compound gate.

"Looks like Oyamo won the argument," said Frank, pulling away from the playful elephant.

"For now," Sammy replied. "But they'll be back.''

The boys finished washing Rafiki, then Sammy gently took hold of the elephant's ear and began pulling her toward the gate of the pen. "I have to take her for a walk to check her limp. Want to come?''

"No, thanks," said Frank. He pulled out the duty list he and Joe had been given earlier. "According to this, I have to bring some supplies over to the lab, and Joe has to help out in the motor pool.''

"Lucky me," the younger Hardy grumbled.

"That's what you get for having a knack for fixing cars," Frank told him. He turned to Sammy. "Is the Masai village far from here?''

"Not really," said Sammy. "It is camouflaged, but with directions you could find it. Another American went there often."

Instantly Frank and Joe became alert.

"What other American?" Joe asked with as much nonchalance as he could muster.

Sammy wrinkled his brow. "Lincoln, I think they called him. He was a photographer."

"Chris Lincoln?" Frank asked, acting more surprised than he really was. "His photographs are famous. Did you know him?"

"Only a little. He came here sometimes to talk to Dr. Bodine and to visit the Masai village."

Sammy paused. "In fact, he was on his way to the Masai village the day he disappeared."

Chapter

6

"CHRIS LINCOLN DISAPPEARED?" Frank asked, trying to sound surprised.

"Yes," Sammy replied. "He stopped by here about a month ago and then left for the Masai village. No one has seen him since. The police have been looking, but without success."

Once more Rafiki tried to grab hold of Frank, causing him to jump to one side. Sammy laughed as he led the elephant away. "She is feeling playful. I had better walk her now."

"It looks as if we should check out the Masai village," Joe said to Frank once Sammy was gone. "But how are we going to get there?"

Frank pulled the duty list from his pocket. "Dr. Bodine has you scheduled to work in the motor pool after lunch. Why don't you keep your eyes peeled for some transportation we can use."

After a hearty meal in the mess hall, the Hardys spent the afternoon on separate assignments. Frank worked with Keir, the Australian, stocking medical supplies and cleaning cages, and Joe went to his assignment in the garage. To his delight, he found two dirt bikes in a corner, both badly in need of tune-ups and one with a flat tire. He soon had the small, two-cylinder engines running smoothly.

He finished an hour before dinner and strode toward the bunkhouse. He noticed Frank talking to Ranger Rawji in the parking lot. When Frank saw Joe, he waved his brother over.

"Ranger Rawji is heading over to the Masai *manyatta*," Frank said.

"*Manyatta* means village, right?" Joe asked.

The ranger smiled at the young man's knowledge of Swahili and nodded.

"It's only a few miles from here," said Frank. "Dr. Bodine says we have time to go before dinner. She said we might learn something."

"Great!" Joe exclaimed. He hoped he and Frank would learn something—about Chris Lincoln's mysterious disappearance.

Minutes later Pope Rawji's jeep was bouncing along a rugged dirt trail that led through rolling, grass-covered hills. The sun was low in the western sky, and the intense heat of midday had given way to warm breezes.

The ranger pointed ahead. "There it is."

Joe leaned forward in his seat. "All I can see are bushes."

The ranger grinned. "That is what you are supposed to see. Look closer."

The *manyatta* was situated in the middle of a grassy plain. As they approached, Frank and Joe saw that the brush was actually a tall fence of twigs and branches encircling thatched huts.

Pope parked his vehicle at an opening in the twig fence. A small elderly man and a thin teenage boy came out to greet them.

"This is Duncan," the ranger said, pointing to the elderly man. "He is much like the official interpreter and spokesman for the village."

"*Jambo,* Ranger Rawji," Duncan said cheerfully. "Who are your friends?"

The ranger introduced Frank and Joe. He heard a crackle of noise from his jeep radio and walked back to the vehicle to take the call.

Duncan placed his hand on the teenager's shoulder. "This is Tenga. He is skilled in the ways of his people."

"The *liabon* says *tayari sasa,*" Tenga told Frank and Joe proudly. "I am ready now."

"A *liabon* is a medicine man," Duncan explained to Frank and Joe. "Tenga is about to become a *moran*—a warrior. In two days he must go into the bush alone and kill a full-grown lion."

Tenga grinned and held his spear proudly over

his head. Frank eyed the Masai teenager. They came from such different worlds, he thought.

Ranger Rawji returned from his jeep. "I have come on business, Duncan. These young men would like to see your *manyatta*. Do you mind?"

Duncan shook his head. "Not at all. We are glad for visitors."

Just then a group of young children gathered around them. They began to tug at Joe, pulling him toward their huts and chanting "*Karibu*."

"*Karibu* means 'welcome,' " Joe said, laughing.

"They want to show you the village," the Masai elder explained.

"I'll stay here," Frank said to Joe. "I want to ask Duncan and Tenga some questions about the village."

Laughing and running ahead of him, the children pulled Joe through the opening in the twig fence. The village was a collection of small brown huts made of dirt and wattle—twigs covered with mud. A large cattle corral was situated in the center. It was empty, which meant the cattle were grazing in fields outside the village. Everything was covered with the dry ash brown dust of the region.

The children led Joe to a hut where a Masai girl with a shy smile showed him carved walking sticks and jewelry. Joe had crouched to enter the low doorway. The inside of the house was small, with a low ceiling and only two tiny windows. It was like stepping back in time. An elderly woman was cooking some type of cereal over a small camp fire.

"*Kwaheri*," Joe said, pronouncing the Swahili word for 'goodbye,' when he was ready to leave. The old woman smiled a toothless smile.

Outside, the children chattered and milled around him. Joe scanned the village for Frank. His brother was nowhere in sight.

Just then someone stepped out of a nearby hut. It was Keesha Imanu!

She was just as surprised to see Joe. "I didn't expect to see you here," she said.

"I came with the ranger," he explained. "I didn't know you were Masai."

"I am not," Keesha said quickly. "I am visiting some of Oyamo's friends. I am from the M'Kamba tribe, near Machakos."

"That's near Nairobi," said Joe. "I remember seeing it on the map. The compound is a long way from your home," he observed.

She nodded. "My village is poor. I have to provide for my family until I marry."

"Oyamo?" Joe asked.

Keesha's eyes flashed. "That is a very personal question."

Joe raised his hands apologetically. "I'm sorry, Keesha. I'm still learning your culture. I didn't mean to offend you."

A faint smile appeared on Keesha's face. "I accept your apology. I have to visit people here before I return to the compound," she said. "We'll talk later, okay?"

"Sure," Joe nodded, waving goodbye.

While Joe was talking with Keesha, Frank walked with Tenga around the perimeter of the *manyatta*. Duncan and the ranger had gone to a hut to talk.

"So you have to kill a lion single-handedly," Frank said, still amazed that African teenagers would take on such a dangerous task. "Is it allowed by the rangers?"

Tenga shook his head no. "But sometimes, the rangers will look a different way and let the Masai follow our ways. Lincoln was to go with me," Tenga said with a hint of sadness. He mimed holding a camera to his eye. "To take pictures. But he has not returned to the *manyatta* for a long time."

Frank stared at the Masai teenager. "You knew Chris Lincoln?"

"*Ndiyo*," Tenga replied, using the Swahili word for "yes." "He is—*rafiki yangu*—my friend. He lived there when he was with the Masai."

Tenga pointed to the shack by the village wall. Unlike the other huts, this was made entirely of grass and branches. It looked like a camper's lean-to.

"He lived here?" Frank asked, suddenly excited.

57

Tenga nodded. "He come, he go. Take pictures."

"Can we go in there?"

Tenga led him over. The shack was only a few feet square inside. Several cowhides had been laid out on the ground to form a bed, and a crudely made shelf was attached to one wall. A bucket filled with dirt served as an ashtray. Frank saw three crushed cigarettes lying on top.

Just then someone in the village shouted Tenga's name. The young Masai gestured that he would be back and stepped outside.

Left alone, Frank began to search the shack. He checked under the cowhides. The shelf held only toothpaste and shaving cream. He knelt to check the cigarettes in the bucket of earth. The ends had been burned down a bit, but they were barely smoked.

For a moment Frank had a sense he had seen cigarettes like these before. Then he remembered—Martin Jellicoe smoked cigarettes like this, taking only a few puffs before throwing them away. As he stood, his foot hit the bucket and knocked it over. Dirt spilled across the cowhides.

Frank leaned over to pick up the bucket and saw something under the remaining earth. He scooped it out. Buried near the bottom were two small plastic bags. One was empty. The other contained a black notebook. Frank opened it and paged through it quickly. Words in a foreign language had been printed in small block letters, page after page.

Suddenly Frank heard Ranger Rawji call his name. He stuffed the notebook into his shirt, scooped the dirt back into the bucket, and replaced the cigarette butts.

Outside, Rawji and Joe waited by the ranger's jeep. Frank was surprised to see Keesha standing with Duncan and several children near the gate. Keesha waved at him and then walked back inside the village.

"She says she'll see us back at the compound later," Joe explained as Frank climbed in. "But we have to go now."

"Yes," said the ranger, "I have work to do." He climbed in and started up the jeep.

"Did you boys have a good visit?" Pope asked as they drove along the rocky trail.

"We sure did," Joe replied.

"Tenga said a photojournalist named Chris Lincoln used to stay at the *manyatta* sometimes," Frank said. "I've seen his photographs in magazines."

Rawji nodded. "The American has not been seen for some time, and the police have been trying to locate him."

"The police!" Frank said with mock surprise. "Are you worried about him?"

"I am concerned," the ranger said calmly. "But I have many more concerns about the animals and poachers, and I do not have time to keep track of human beings."

The jeep crested a hill. Off to the left Frank could see a small water hole surrounded by trees.

"See that?" Rawji said, and pointed. "We have not had rain in some time, and water is scarce. That is one of the last water holes before the barren country. Animals go there to drink in the morning and at night. Unfortunately, because the animals have only a few places to go for water, the poachers know where to strike."

Ranger Rawji faced the Hardys. "And therefore, to capture poachers, so do we."

The ranger was quiet throughout the rest of the ride to the compound. When he dropped the Hardys off, twilight was gathering. It would soon be dark. Joe checked his watch.

"Barely in time for dinner," he announced, glancing over at the mess hall. Joe was never one to miss a meal.

"Hold it," Frank told him. "I found something important in a lean-to that Lincoln used at the *manyatta*." He showed Joe the notebook.

"Incredible!" Joe exclaimed, reaching for it. "Let's look it over."

"Dinner first." Frank laughed, surprised that Joe had forgotten food so quickly.

An hour later, their stomachs full from an excellent meal, Frank and Joe walked across the

60

compound from the mess hall to the dormitory. The eerie sounds of weaver birds and baboons filled the night air. There was no moon, and darkness hung over the compound like a thick curtain.

The other guests had gone to the recreation hall to watch television or play Ping-Pong, leaving the Hardys alone in the bunkhouse. They pulled out the two plastic bags Frank had found. Frank took the book from one and opened it. "It's in a foreign language," he said.

"Or code," Joe pointed out, trying to read the tiny writing. "At least, it doesn't look like any language I know. How long will it take you to figure it out?"

Frank grinned. "Thanks for the vote of confidence, Joe, but I have no idea. It would be easier if we had a computer to run it through."

Frank picked up the empty plastic bag, opened it, and took a deep breath. "There's the faint smell of gun powder," he said quietly. "I bet Lincoln kept a gun in this bag."

"Let's reconstruct what happened," Joe suggested. "First Lincoln comes here to the compound, then he goes out to the Masai village."

"He hides this notebook and takes his gun from its hiding place," Frank continued.

"Because he was expecting to run into trouble," Joe interrupted.

"He was probably going after the poachers,"

Frank said. "But where? If we knew where they were going to strike next, we might get a lead."

Joe snapped his fingers. "Maybe we do! Ranger Rawji told us that water hole was a prime spot for poachers to go after animals. Want to go out there and take a look?"

"How do we get there?" Frank asked.

"No problem," Joe said with a grin. "I tuned up a couple of old dirt bikes this afternoon because I thought we'd need them to get to the Masai village. We'll take those."

Frank hid the notebook in his duffel bag and followed Joe to the garage on the other side of the bunkhouse. The building was deserted. Joe led Frank to the back where the bikes were ready on their stands.

"What do we say if we're caught with these?" Frank wondered out loud.

"I told the mechanic that I'd test them," Joe said. "Now's as good a time as any."

The Hardys walked the bikes quietly down the drive and onto the road. Just outside the gate, they kicked the starters and revved the engines. A moment later they were on the road to the water hole. The night was still moonless, brightened only by stars, and the unfamiliar terrain forced them to ride slowly.

The cool night air felt good against Joe's face, and the dirt bikes handled the rough, rutted road easily. Their headlights just outlined a deep ravine off to their right. As they neared the water hole, everything seemed quiet and calm.

Frank and Joe were moving through a cluster of trees as their headlights picked out a group of men by the edge of the water. Four of them, in ranger uniforms, had their hands in the air. They were surrounded by other men armed with rifles. Everyone turned toward the bright headlights and the sound of the engines. Two men leveled their rifles at the Hardys and took aim.

"Look out!" Frank shouted.

The night grew bright with flashes of blue light. Bullets cut the air.

Turning the wheels of their bikes sharply, Frank and Joe careened off the road—and plunged into the blackness of the deep ravine!

Chapter
7

JOE'S BODY HIT the ground with a bone-jarring impact. His bare arms scraped across the rocks as he tumbled to the bottom of the ravine. He looked up in time to see Frank rolling through a tangle of dry brush and thorns. Somewhere below them the motorbikes crashed. The engines screamed and died. Volleys of gunfire still rang out in the night from the watering hole.

Joe stumbled to his feet just as Frank rolled out of the bushes, his shirt and pants torn from the fall.

"Anything broken?" Joe asked.

"No," Frank said, gasping for air. He rose painfully to his feet. "Come on."

They scrambled up the steep incline until they were almost at the top. Clinging to the side of the ravine for cover, the Hardys peered over the edge.

It seemed that the rangers had taken advantage of the Hardys' unexpected arrival. They had managed to snatch up rifles, and spread out, and were now exchanging shots with the poachers. Bright flashes of gunfire blinked like strobe lights. Frank and Joe caught glimpses of the rangers, outlined against their muzzle flashes.

Single-shot rifle fire was answered by the rapid, muffled cough of deadly assault rifles, spitting bullets.

"The rangers don't have a chance." Joe scanned the battle zone. He spotted the dark shape of a poacher, creeping carefully along the edge of the ravine to move up behind the rangers. The man had a rifle.

"He's got his back to us," Joe whispered to Frank. "Let's nail him."

Frank nodded. "Give me a second to distract him."

He moved quickly along the incline of the ravine until he was almost even with the poacher. Then he jumped up over the edge, shouting. The poacher turned toward him, firing almost instantly but missing Frank, who had rolled to cover.

Hearing the disturbance, a ranger turned to fire at the poacher. His gun clicked on an empty chamber. The poacher stood and turned back to the ranger, his automatic rifle raised.

Joe sprinted over the edge of the ravine and pounced like a panther. He caught the poacher at the knees and pulled him to the ground, desperately pushing the barrel of the rifle away from himself.

The two rose to their feet, locked in a deadly hug. Gripping the barrel, Joe pushed the rifle away with his left hand and reared back and fired a hard right jab to the poacher's face. The man lost his grip on the gun and fell.

Joe shouted and threw the gun to Frank. Two more poachers left the underbrush and took aim across the clearing. A ranger opened fire on them before they could close in. Wounded, one of the poachers dropped his rifle and fled.

Joe's opponent was disarmed but not out. He stood and swung at Joe's head. Joe successfully blocked it, but didn't see the poacher raise his leg to kick him in the side. Joe groaned and doubled over in pain. Slowly he dropped to the ground, gasping for breath. His assailant pulled out a knife and stepped forward.

Suddenly the barrel of a rifle came out of the night, snapping across the man's wrist and knocking the knife from his hand. He turned to face his new opponent, just in time to receive a roundhouse kick to the jaw from Frank. The poacher froze, teetered for a moment, and tumbled over. He remained perfectly still.

"You okay?" Frank called to his brother.

"I am now." Joe scrambled to his feet.

The gunfire and fighting had stopped. They heard shouts and the sound of car engines revving up.

"Come on!" Frank shouted.

They ran in the direction of the noise and stumbled into a clearing, where the rangers were firing at several trucks that fled rapidly into the distance with their lights out. The rangers stopped shooting and lowered their guns as the vehicles disappeared into the blackness of night.

"That's Rawji," Joe said to Frank, pointing at one of the rangers. Starlight from the clear sky overhead provided them with just enough visibility to recognize the head ranger.

The Hardys ran over to him. "Are you all right?" Frank asked.

"You are the ones on the dirt bikes!" he exclaimed when he saw the brothers.

"We were out for a ride and stumbled into this," Frank said, glancing at Joe.

"They were about to kill us," Rawji said. "You saved our lives."

"Why don't you chase them?" Joe asked.

"They disabled our vehicles."

"Well, they left this behind." Frank handed Rawji the assault rifle. The ranger took it, his hand shaking with rage. "These guns are weapons of war! How are we to fight men like this?"

"At least we got one of them." Joe told Rawji about the unconscious man. The ranger waved over two of his men and sent them to handcuff him.

Rawji pointed to a stand of trees. "Our jeeps are hidden over there. Please bring both first-aid kits. Some of my men are hurt."

Frank and Joe raced to the rangers' vehicles and returned with first-aid kits. Quickly Frank and the rangers bandaged the wounded men while Rawji and Joe checked out the jeeps. The poachers had yanked the wires from the distributor in each vehicle, but it took Joe only a few minutes to repair them. The Hardys agreed to abandon the wrecked dirt bikes in the ravine until daylight. They headed back to the compound with the rangers.

On the drive Frank looked over the assault rifle they had captured. "This is a nine-millimeter automatic carbine," he said. "NATO forces use them. But this one is fitted with an illegal silencer."

Joe was amazed. "I'd figured the poachers had firepower, but this is enough to fight a small war."

"Or even a big one," Frank added. "These guys are equipped."

"But where would they get guns like this out here, in the middle of nowhere?" Joe wondered.

"It's only about three and a half hours to Nairobi," Rawji told them. "And less to Mombasa. There have been rumors of weapons being smuggled into the port there."

Frank held the automatic carbine out for Joe and Rawji to see. He pointed to a spot of rough metal on the underside of the barrel. "Too bad they've filed off the serial numbers."

Instead of looking at the gun, Rawji looked at the Hardys. "You do not sound typical of the young people who come to work for Dr. Bodine," he said finally.

Frank laughed to dispel the ranger's suspicion. "You can learn a lot from watching American TV."

They rode in silence until they reached the Bodine Animal Research Compound. Ranger Rawji walked Frank and Joe into Rosalyn Bodine's office. The veterinarian, her eyes red and tired, was doing paperwork at her desk.

"They saved our lives, Dr. Bodine," Ranger Rawji concluded after telling his story. "If Frank and Joe had not chosen this late hour to test-drive those dirt bikes, I and my men would not be here now."

Rosalyn Bodine's expression was impossible to read. She had remained impassive behind her desk and seemed upset only when she heard about the shooting. Even Joe's tale about taking the bikes out for a test drive hadn't roused much reaction.

"Were any leopards hurt?" she asked finally.

"No," said Rawji. "We drove the animals off before the poachers arrived."

"Well, thank goodness for that, if nothing

else," she said in an exasperated voice. She turned to the Hardys. "I'd like to talk to Ranger Rawji alone," she said. "I'll see you two in the morning. I suggest you get some sleep. I'm going to Mombasa tomorrow with Oyamo and Keesha to pick up some sick animals at a warehouse. I want both of you to come with us. That way I can keep an eye on you."

Frank and Joe started to leave.

"Asante sana, Frank and Joe," Rawji said sincerely. It meant "thank you."

"You're welcome," Joe replied with a smile.

Frank and Joe headed for the bunkhouse. As they walked across the compound, a baboon screeched from a nearby tree. His call sounded like a twisted, maniacal laugh.

"Whose side are you on?" Joe mumbled to the trees. "Theirs or ours?" He paused, peering into the dark branches, hoping to spot the animal. After a few minutes he gave up and followed Frank to the bunkhouse.

His brother was waiting for him outside the door, holding the notebook he had found in Lincoln's lean-to at the Masai village. Frank pulled a penlight from his pocket.

"Let's take a look at this and see if we can figure it out," he said, opening the book and shining the light on the first page.

Strange words were spread across the page.

ODNOKO LGOOKNO DMAU MYBUNU ASBMI
SKAMAI TYNAI IFSI MYNEARE AGKAN
NEGED. MOTEB AFRIKU KMAISMA TAGWI
AKPA URCHA

A quick glance through the rest of the notebook showed that the whole thing was written
in the same language.

Joe shrugged. "I'm pretty sure it's not Swahili," he said. "Maybe it's some other African
language."

Frank nodded. After taking a pen and a piece
of blank notepaper from the back of the book,
he copied down the first three lines. "Maybe we
can find someone in Mombasa tomorrow who
can translate some of it, or at least tell us what
language it is."

The following morning the sun was hot before
they left the compound. Frank and Joe rode with
Sammy in one of two pickup trucks. The lead
truck carried Oyamo, Keesha, and Dr. Bodine.
For several hours they drove east on a modern
paved highway and finally rolled across a bridge
into Mombasa at eleven o'clock. The air was
thick with moisture. The trucks weren't air-con-
ditioned, and Frank's shirt was sticky with
sweat.

"We will be at the docks in a few minutes,"
Sammy said.

71

"How many animals are we picking up?" Frank asked.

"Only a few," Sammy replied. "We do this quite often. Zoos and parks send us their sick ones."

"So where are the bathing beauties?" Joe Hardy demanded, leaning out the window as they drove down Jomo Kenyatta Avenue.

"You will have to go over to the beaches for that," Sammy replied.

"Over?" said Joe. "What do you mean?"

Sammy laughed. "The city of Mombasa is on an island," he explained. "The beaches are on the mainland coast that surrounds it. The warehouse is on the east end of the island near the old town. There are no bikini ladies there."

"Just great," Joe muttered, visibly disappointed.

Mombasa was a small, bustling city. Much of it seemed lost in time. Two-story shops and weathered apartment houses squatted along the streets, their white and blue paint faded by years of blazing sunlight.

They arrived at Dhow Docks and cruised along a row of warehouses that lined a wharf stretching out into the water. They stopped in front of the last and largest one.

" 'Phoenix Enterprises,' " Joe read aloud from the sign across the front of the building. " 'Importing and Exporting since 1965.' "

The lead truck had arrived several minutes before they did, and was parked in front of the warehouse.

"Looks as if there's a problem," Frank said. He saw Dr. Bodine arguing with a large man at the door of the warehouse.

"That is Rashid," Sammy said. "He is the warehouse manager for Phoenix Enterprises."

The Hardys leapt from the truck and strode over to the doctor.

"I cannot help what the planes do," Rashid was saying as they approached. He had a thick Middle Eastern accent and puffed on a strong-smelling cigarette wrapped in brown tobacco like a thin cigar. He was overweight, with jet black hair and a thick mustache. His eyes were watery, and his rumpled clothes stained with spots.

Rosalyn Bodine frowned. "Rashid, how long a delay are you talking about?"

The warehouse manager puffed on his strange cigarette and exhaled a thick cloud of smoke. "They said maybe two hours."

Rosalyn turned toward the group. "All right, everyone, there's nothing we can do but wait." She turned to Frank and Joe. "You two can browse if you want, but keep out of trouble."

A few minutes later the Hardys were strolling along the narrow, rutted streets of Mombasa's Old Town. Two-story stone buildings lined the streets. Some were decorated with ornately carved wooden doors and brackets; others had balconies and shutters. Frank noticed a small restaurant. He was about to suggest they stop for a cola when a street peddler stepped from behind a wagon filled with fruits and vegetables.

"Good mango, *bwana*. You buy, ten shillings." The dark-skinned peddler wore a turban and grinned happily, even though he was missing most of his front teeth.

"No, thanks," Joe said. He tried to think of the right words in Swahili. "Uh, *hapana*—"

Suddenly he felt something hard push against his side. He glanced down. The peddler was jabbing a gun into his ribs.

Joe swallowed. "Careful," he said calmly. "They're still sore from last night." He nodded at Frank, who froze as he stared at the peddler.

"Please to turn down this alley," the man said in an icy tone. His dark eyes narrowed, and he wiped a dirty hand across his unshaven cheek. "Both of you," he demanded, jabbing the gun harder into Joe's side.

"And if we don't?" Frank asked, stalling.

"Then the inevitable will happen that much sooner," the man sneered.

The Hardys moved slowly down the narrow street, looking for an opportunity to escape while the peddler nudged them forward with the long barrel of his gun. The street ended in a small, dingy courtyard. A canvas-topped truck waited with the motor running.

The peddler steered Frank and Joe toward the

tailgate. A hand reached through the canvas flap and threw it open. Another man, shorter and fatter than the peddler, stood inside. He wore grease-covered overalls and also held a gun.

"Get in!" he growled, his dark eyes cold and glinting.

The peddler nudged them fròm behind. The Hardys climbed into the back of the truck and sat on a bench along one side. The second gunman sat opposite them, eyeing them impassively with empty eyes. He kept his gun pointed at Joe, who was closer to the tailgate.

"Please do not try any stunts," the peddler said, peering at them from outside the truck. "My friend would prefer not to change his plans."

Frank stared into the first gunman's dark, brooding eyes. "What are his plans?"

The peddler cackled. "Once we are out of the city, he is going to slit your throats."

Chapter

8

JOE'S EYES NARROWED. "You've got a lousy sense of humor," he said, gritting his teeth. He was tensed, his fists clenched, ready to spring.

"That would not be a good thing to do." The peddler raised his gun.

Frank grabbed Joe's shoulder, and his brother sat back, breathing hard.

"Much better," the peddler said. He dropped the flap down over the back of the truck, walked around to the front, and jumped in the cab with the driver. With the transmission roaring in first gear, the truck pulled out of the courtyard.

It was impossible for Frank to see where they were going. A small window in the back of the cab allowed them only a view of their captors' heads. The back of the truck was completely covered in a military green canvas. The lumbering vehicle took a number of sharp turns. Then he heard the sound of wheels on gratings and boat whistles. They were going back over the bridge from Mombasa to the mainland. The truck turned again and picked up speed.

"You guys have made a mistake," Frank called to the men in the cab.

The peddler leered at them through the back window. "Oh, no. That is not the case. You and your associates have come to interfere with our employer's business. This is not allowed."

The flap over the tailgate blew open, and Joe saw a country road. Trees and tall grass raced past on either side. The truck began a slow climb up a steep hill, its gears straining with the effort. The truck was lumbering from side to side over potholes and cracks.

The peddler's face appeared again in the cab window. "This is the road to Malindi and Lamu," he explained. "They have lovely beaches and pretty ladies. Too bad you will not see them. When we are farther into the bush, we will finish our business with you."

The gunman opposite the Hardys grinned wickedly.

"I don't think he's been fed," Frank murmured to Joe from the side of his mouth. This was their last chance to escape, and he knew it. He wiped sweat from his brow using only two fingers. It was a signal to Joe that they would make a move.

Frank leaned toward the cabin window as if to speak to the peddler. At the same time Joe edged away from Frank and leaned slightly in the opposite direction.

The truck suddenly jolted to one side for a split second, throwing the gunman momentarily off-balance. The Hardys reacted, coming at him from both sides.

Joe grabbed the gunman's hand and slammed it down across a crate as Frank threw a hard left jab to the man's nose. His eyes rolled up into his head, and he sank to his knees. The gun flew against the canvas side and fell behind some boxes. Joe leapt out the back of the truck with Frank on his heels.

They rolled onto the road after leaping from the moving truck to ease the force of their fall. Then they leapt to their feet and raced into the jungle. Joe hoped the gunman couldn't get to his weapon before they reached it.

"This way!" Frank yelled, jumping a log and ducking under low-hanging branches. On the road the truck screeched to a halt. They heard shouts and the sounds of men racing after them.

"We can lose them in this thick growth," Frank said, running faster.

Suddenly the trees ended abruptly at the edge of a river. A roaring waterfall plummeted thirty feet into a lush ravine.

"What were you saying about losing them?" Joe panted, surveying the impasse.

Frank peered down at the water. Behind him the sounds of their pursuers crashing through the bush grew louder. "Let's do it!" he shouted.

Bullets popped, and the air whistled beside Joe's head. He leapt out into space, dimly aware of Frank in the air beside him. His stomach twisted as he fell into the frothing waters below the falls.

The stream was cold, but the water clear. Bullets exploded around them. Joe felt Frank's hand clutch his arm and pull him down farther. Frank motioned underwater. Holding their breath and each other, they let the river's strong current carry them downstream. When their lungs were screaming for oxygen, they rose to the surface and gulped in fresh air.

Joe was slammed against a rock and gagged. Frank swam up beside him.

"You need help?" he sputtered.

Joe shook his head and waved toward shore. "Save your breath. Let's swim for it."

"Piece of cake," Frank gasped, setting out with a strong freestyle stroke.

Five minutes later, when they pulled themselves onto the riverbank, Frank raised his hand for silence. The forest was quiet, their pursuers nowhere in sight.

"They must have been following us in Mombasa," Joe panted. "Someone tipped them off about us."

"They weren't the same guys we saw last night," said Frank. "Those were Africans. These guys looked Arab or East Indian."

"The peddler said something about his friends in the bush," Joe reminded Frank.

"That's right," Frank agreed. "And if they're coming after us, we must be getting close to something." He looked grimly at Joe. "I hate to think what might have happened to Agent Lincoln."

Joe nodded. "I've been thinking the same thing. It looks as if these poachers will stop at nothing. I'd hate to be the one to have to tell Congressman Alladyce that his best friend didn't make it."

Frank stood. "Now all we have to do is find our way back to the warehouse."

"Or the beach," Joe said, rubbing his hands together. "Whichever comes first."

They made their way slowly through the underbrush and soon stumbled across the highway.

"I guess we'll have to walk back to Mombasa," Frank said.

"No way," Joe said. He pointed far down the road, where a pickup truck with a camper top on the back was fast approaching. "I bet that's a *matatu*."

"A what?"

"A *matatu*—a bus." Joe grinned. "According

to my Swahili guidebook, they run all along the roads in Kenya. Let's flag it down.''

Five minutes later the Hardys were in the back of the pickup on their way into Mombasa. There were already ten people crowded aboard when Frank and Joe climbed in, and the driver kept stopping to cram more and more into the tiny space.

"Would you please get your elbow out of my face?" Frank complained.

Joe tried to shift around, but there was no room.

"Well, it's a great way to get to know people," Joe said cheerfully.

Half an hour later the *matatu* dropped them off only blocks from the Phoenix warehouse in Mombasa. Barely two hours had elapsed since they had set off on their stroll through the old town. Their clothing was almost dry, but dirty and torn.

As the Hardys approached the warehouse, they saw Rosalyn Bodine talking with Rashid again. She didn't appear to be any happier now than she had been the first time.

"If I'd known there was going to be this kind of delay, I would have gone to the airfield myself," she stormed.

The foreman seemed undisturbed by her anger. "That's impossible. The airport is private." He lit another cigarette. "I am truly sorry for the delay."

"You say it will be another hour?" Dr. Bodine asked.

"Only one more, I assure you." Rashid smiled. He puffed on his cigarette and breathed a pungent cloud of smoke into the air. The veterinarian turned away in frustration and spotted Frank and Joe.

Frank saw her gasp, but he noticed that Rashid reacted even more. The Phoenix manager flinched. His eyes grew wide, then darkened.

"What happened to you two *this* time?" Dr. Bodine demanded.

Frank glanced down at his grimy clothes. "We got into a game of—uh, soccer over at the park."

Dr. Bodine shook her head. "I pity your parents." She studied the boys for a moment. "You obviously heard about the added delay. You might as well come and have some lunch with me. If they'll let you in a restaurant."

Rosalyn Bodine drove them to the Castle Hotel. The building was painted bright white, with natural wood beams supporting a shingled awning. A small wrought-iron fence separated a pleasant restaurant from the sidewalk.

"This looks a lot like our hotel in Nairobi," Frank commented.

"It's the same Victorian influence," Dr. Bodine explained. She ordered a salad and wine for herself. "I'm a vegetarian," she declared. "So please don't order anything that's still bleeding."

The Hardys ordered tuna sandwiches and ice-cold lemonade.

"All right," she announced once the food had arrived. "What are you two all about?"

Frank and Joe just looked at her.

"Don't give me that I'm-too-innocent-for-words look," Dr. Bodine threw back at them. "I've lived among animals all my life, and I've learned to trust my instincts. Perhaps I should remind you, people are animals, too."

"What makes you think we're up to anything?" Frank asked.

She began counting off with the fingers of one hand. "Since you arrived, there's been a snake in Frank's bed—"

"Someone put that in his bed," Joe interrupted defensively.

"And you"—she turned to the younger Hardy and counted on her second finger—"you nearly got hanged."

"We were chasing poachers," Joe replied. His hand unconsciously went to his neck, which still displayed a red, raw, rope burn.

Rosalyn Bodine's green eyes narrowed. "Newcomers don't go running into the bush chasing men with guns. They're usually too scared of the animals, let alone the human danger."

"Sammy and Oyamo went into the bush first," Joe pointed out.

"That doesn't matter." Dr. Bodine leaned

back in her chair. Bright African sunlight glinted on her blond hair.

"And that brings us to last night," Dr. Bodine continued. "You not only went out on your own, at night, but when you ran into gunfire, you fought back."

Joe bit into his sandwich and avoided the veterinarian's piercing eyes.

"You're either major troublemakers," Bodine concluded, "or you're after something. What is it?"

Frank sighed and glanced at Joe. "We're looking for a friend of ours," he said. "A man named Chris Lincoln."

Dr. Bodine's eyes widened.

"He's disappeared," Joe said quickly. "No one seems to be able to find him, and no one seems to care. So we decided to look for him ourselves."

Rosalyn sipped her wine slowly, never taking her eyes off the boys. "Why didn't you say so in the beginning?"

"We didn't want people telling us to mind our own business," Joe said.

"And we didn't want to be asked to leave— by you or the authorities," Frank added.

"We know he visited the research compound," Joe said. "Do you have any idea where he might be?"

Rosalyn Bodine nibbled on her salad. She seemed deep in thought, and when she finally spoke, she chose her words carefully. "I don't know where he is, but I'm afraid he's in trouble. He asked too many questions, in the wrong places, about the wrong people. About poaching. And believe me, the men involved in that kind of savagery are bad news. They'd kill a person as fast as they kill innocent animals."

"Chris was a photojournalist," Joe said. "He was looking for a good story."

"Did Chris tell you anything about the compound?" the doctor asked.

"That you were doing some great work," Frank answered earnestly.

"He also said money was scarce," Joe prodded.

Rosalyn laughed. "Scarce. Chris was understating the situation. In about twenty years several species integral to this world's survival will become extinct. And still people are paying enormous amounts of money for illegal elephant ivory, rhinoceros horns, and leopard skins. Poachers will lie, steal, and kill to get hold of these things." She looked away, her expression sad.

"Where should we look for Chris?" Joe asked softly. "Do you have any idea?"

The question seemed to pull Dr. Bodine from her thoughts.

"He spent a lot of time with the Masai," she told them. "He picked up their habit of walking all over the countryside. Said it helped him to sneak up on wildlife more easily.''

It also enabled him to sneak up on poachers, Frank thought, remembering the videotape Congressman Alladyce had shown them in New York.

''I feel like we're losing the battle to save these animals,'' Rosalyn confessed. ''Money is winning, not the planet.'' She sipped the last of her wine. ''Boys, let the police look for your friend. I'd hate to see anything happen to you.''

When they returned to the Phoenix warehouse, Sammy, Keesha, and Oyamo were waiting. Rashid informed them that the truck would be there in a few minutes.

''While we have a minute, let's call that contact number Dad gave us,'' Frank suggested to Joe. ''We should bring him up to date.''

The Hardys strolled up the block until they found a pay phone. Both had memorized the telephone number. Frank dialed and heard it ring four times. A man answered.

Frank asked to speak to Fenton Hardy. There was a long pause, and some strange noises in the background. Abruptly, and to Frank's surprise, his father came on the line.

''Good to hear from you,'' Fenton said. ''Things are moving fast at my end.''

''Same here,'' said Frank. He brought his father up to date and concluded, ''The notebook is the only solid clue we've found.''

"That's good work, son," Fenton Hardy said warmly. "If it's in code, see what you can do to crack it." Then he sounded concerned. "It looks as if your cover has been blown. You and Joe could be sitting ducks out there at the compound."

"We'll be careful, Dad," Frank reassured him. "If we're dangerous enough for them to try to get rid of us, we must be getting close. We're just not sure what—or who—it is yet."

"Son, the stakes are higher than we thought," Fenton told Frank. "My own contacts have proof that payoffs have been made on a very high level. They've also heard rumors of heavier muscle coming in."

"That ties in with what happened to us," Frank said. "The automatic weapons we ran across and the guys who kidnapped us."

"There's also a rumor that smugglers may be dealing in more than animals. What you've told me about the assault rifles gives me another angle."

"When do you meet with this contact again?" Frank asked.

"A member of the smuggling ring has promised me a load of ivory in a few days. He also said there might be some leopard skins."

"Be careful, Dad," Frank said.

"I will," Fenton replied. "Call if you need me." Then he hung up.

Frank placed the receiver back in its cradle.

"Dad's getting in deeper," he told Joe. "And he's doing it alone."

Joe nodded. "There's always one of us to back the other up, but no one's covering Dad."

"If his cover is blown, he's a dead man," Frank concluded grimly.

Chapter
9

FRANK AND JOE walked back down the street to the warehouse and arrived just as the Phoenix truck finally drove up. A short, elderly man sat behind the wheel.

"Come on," said Frank. "Let's help load the animals."

There were only three cages. Two baboons were suffering from a flu, while a baby ostrich had injured one of its long, powerful legs. Joe helped load Rosalyn's truck while Frank worked with Sammy. When they placed the last cage onto the truck, Joe saw Rashid wave Dr. Bodine over to the entrance of the warehouse.

Casually Joe followed the veterinarian over and stood next to her. Another cigarette dangled from the corner of the warehouse manager's mouth. Joe wrinkled his nose against the strong smell.

"Please sign here for the animals." Rashid exhaled a cloud of foul smoke. "As usual, the government of Kenya must receive many copies of the health certificate for their records." He handed Rosalyn a clipboard and a pen.

Joe noticed that the form on the clipboard contained many multi-colored sheets layered with carbon paper. He watched as Dr. Bodine scrawled her name across the bottom line after barely glancing at the top sheet.

"I don't have time for all this paperwork," she said with annoyance. "But without this form, those animals can't go anywhere, can they?"

The veterinarian handed the clipboard back to Rashid. "I want to examine one of those baboons before we leave. It looks more ill than I was told."

Dr. Bodine turned and strode back to the truck. Joe hung back, standing just outside the door of the warehouse. He watched Rashid flip through the layers of the form and saw a tiny smile play across the warehouse manager's swarthy face. Unaware of Joe's presence, Rashid set the clipboard down on a desk just inside the door and retreated into the warehouse. Joe watched him disappear behind a long row of crates.

Joe eased into the warehouse and stood over

the desk, scanning the Veterinary Health Certificate. It documented that two baboons and an ostrich had been shipped and listed the owners and the health condition of the animals. Dr. Bodine's signature was at the bottom beside an official seal.

Joe shot a quick glance around the loading area. Rashid was nowhere to be seen, and the other workers were busy securing the animals in the trucks. Cautiously he lifted the first page of the certificate and the carbon paper underneath it.

The second page appeared identical to the first and was dated for the same day. But it wasn't an exact duplicate. Instead of two baboons and an ostrich, it listed several leopards and exotic birds. The carbon impression of Dr. Bodine's signature made it look completely official.

Joe flipped through the rest of the duplicate papers. All had copies of Dr. Bodine's signature—and a different list of animals. He heard footsteps in the warehouse. Rashid was returning. Quickly Joe headed back outside.

He walked over to the second truck, where Dr. Bodine and Oyamo were examining a sickly baboon. "This animal will make it," she said. "But we've got to get her to the compound immediately."

Joe saw Rashid come around the end of the truck, holding his clipboard again.

"I trust all is in order now, Doctor," the foreman said pleasantly.

"We have to get the animals back to the compound," Rosalyn replied sternly. "The delay hasn't been easy on them."

"Everything is in order," Rashid said. Joe saw him tear off the top page of the health certificate and hand it to the doctor. "I look forward to seeing you all again."

The veterinarian folded it without a second look and tucked it in her shirt pocket. She climbed into the lead truck with Keesha and Oyamo, while the Hardys climbed into the second one beside Sammy. Soon they were on their way.

Joe could barely contain himself on the long drive from Mombasa back to the Bodine Animal Research Compound. He didn't dare say anything to Frank until they were alone. It was almost late afternoon before the trucks finally drove through the gates and parked outside the animal hospital. When the animals had been unloaded, Joe tugged at Frank's shirtsleeve.

"Let's take a walk," he said. He led his brother toward Rafiki's corral. Except for the elephant, they were completely alone. Rafiki greeted them by raising her trunk and trumpeting. Then she went back to munching contentedly on a pile of hay.

"Did you find out anything?" Frank asked.

Joe beamed and nodded. He told Frank about

the duplicate health certificate. "Dr. Bodine barely paid any attention to what she was signing," he explained. "Instead of making duplicate copies, they've tricked her into signing several different certificates. Then they must use them to smuggle live animals through customs and make it all look legal."

"So without Dr. Bodine knowing it, she's become involved in smuggling animals," Frank concluded. He slammed his fist into the palm of his other hand. "Finally we've started to crack this case! Phoenix Enterprises is in it up to their necks."

Joe nodded. "But we still don't know what happened to Chris Lincoln," he reminded Frank.

"That's right," Frank agreed. "And that's why Congressman Alladyce brought us in on this case. We still have some work to do, little brother."

Just then Keesha walked onto the porch of the main house and called toward them.

"There is a telephone call waiting for you," she said, descending the steps and approaching the brothers. "A man asked for either Frank or Joe."

"Maybe it's Dad," Joe said. "We should fill him in on this."

"You take it," Frank said. "I'll wait out here."

Joe ran across the grass and climbed the steps to the porch. Keesha strolled over to Rafiki's corral. She reached into a large brown bag she carried and threw a handful of peanuts at the elephant. Rafiki immediately ignored the hay and came toward Keesha, reaching for the brown bag with her trunk.

"She likes peanuts, I guess," Frank said, smiling at Keesha.

The young woman looked at Frank bashfully. "It's her last day here," she said. "In another hour we're releasing her into a herd nearby."

"Will the herd take back an elephant that's been raised mostly by humans?"

"Many times, yes," Keesha replied. "But we have a special situation this time. One of the adult females in the herd was also raised by Dr. Bodine. We hope she will come out of the herd to welcome Rafiki and take her back with her."

"They really take care of each other that much?" Frank asked. "That's hard to believe."

Keesha smiled slightly. "Before I came here, I would have thought so, too. But I have come to learn they are quite intelligent and just as social as humans are."

Frank gently pushed Rafiki's trunk away from his ear and patted the white, arrow-shaped birthmark on the young elephant's forehead. The young elephant made a faint trumpeting sound and rested her trunk on Frank's shoulder. Just then Dr. Bodine approached the corral from the direction of the animal hospital.

"She seems to like you," Rosalyn said, glancing at Rafiki. "Why don't you and your brother come with us when we set her free?"

"Sounds good to me," Frank replied. Gazing past Dr. Bodine, he saw Joe leave the main house. "I'm sure Joe will want to come."

"Fine," said the doctor. "We leave in a few minutes. It will soon be dusk, and the herd likes to gather at a nearby stream around this time of day."

Dr. Bodine turned and headed for the house, Keesha following. They gave Joe a friendly greeting when they passed.

"What's up?" Joe asked his brother when he reached the corral.

"We've been invited to go with Dr. Bodine when she takes Rafiki back to the herd. We leave in a few minutes."

Joe grinned. "Your first date. That's nice."

Frank jabbed his brother's arm. "Was it Dad on the phone?"

Joe shook his head. "It was Jellicoe, just checking up on us. I told him about the men who tried to abduct us in Mombasa, and he seemed concerned. He said he's going to report to Assistant Commissioner Daly. He says it's getting too dangerous for us."

"Did you mention Dad?"

Joe frowned and shook his head. "No, but Jellicoe did. Dad still hasn't contacted him. I'm worried."

Frank nodded slowly. "I am, too. It seems

strange Dad hasn't talked to Jellicoe yet. Maybe we should use the phone number to call him again."

Just then the Hardys heard Sammy calling. He was at the wheel of a jeep parked outside the big house. Dr. Bodine strode purposefully across the porch. She had changed into a safari jacket and hiking boots.

"When we get back," Joe said. "Right now we have a date with an elephant."

Half an hour later Joe was crouched next to Frank in tall, dry grass upwind of a narrow, muddy stream. Sammy parked the jeep a few dozen yards behind them and joined them in the grass. A large elephant herd was barely fifty feet away, with beasts of all ages drinking at the edge of a water hole.

Across the clearing, several hundred feet away on the other side of the herd, Dr. Bodine stood with Oyamo and Keesha. Rafiki was between them, using her trunk to play with Oyamo and ignoring the herd.

As Joe and Frank watched, an enormous female elephant left the bank of the stream and began walking toward the veterinarian and her workers. The elephant lifted her trunk and trumpeted into the air. Dr. Bodine stepped forward to greet the great beast, stroking the animal's trunk and speaking into its ear.

"Incredible," Joe said to Frank. "That elephant just walked up to Doc Bodine like they were old friends."

"They are old friends." Sammy grinned. "Dr. Bodine raised that elephant, too, and released it to the herd two years ago."

Rosalyn Bodine turned and signaled to Oyamo. The foreman swatted Rafiki's rump. The elephant stepped forward, looking from Dr. Bodine to the larger elephant beside her, as if she were confused. Oyamo swatted Rafiki again, and again the young female took a few steps.

Soon the two elephants were standing side by side. Bodine stroked Rafiki's side. The other elephant raised her trunk and trumpeted loudly again, waving her trunk toward the rest of the herd. Dr. Bodine pushed Rafiki forward. Slowly at first, then faster, Rafiki followed the other elephant to the stream. A moment later the herd closed around her.

"Amazing," Joe said, shaking his head in disbelief. "These animals are a lot more intelligent than most people give them credit for."

Frank nodded vaguely. He sniffed at the air. "You smell smoke?"

Joe followed his brother's lead and sniffed, too. "Something's burning," he agreed.

Sammy poked his head above the grass. Suddenly some elephants in the herd began trumpeting with alarm.

Frank turned around. Not far from where Dr. Bodine had been standing with Oyamo and

Keesha, thick clouds of black smoke rose above bright red flames. The tall, dry grass was ablaze.

"Fire!" Sammy yelled with horror.

"And it's moving this way!" Frank shouted.

"That's not the only thing moving this way," Joe said, pointing toward the stream.

The elephant herd was panicking. Dozens of twenty-ton animals were moving toward them, running faster and faster to escape the smoke and flames.

"The herd is stampeding!" Joe shouted. "And we're right in their path!"

Chapter

10

A WALL OF GRAY DEATH thundered toward the Hardys at a frightening speed. Trees cracked and splintered as the herd smashed through the bush, madly trumpeting their fear.

"This way!" Joe shouted to Frank and Sammy. "We can't outrun them. Our only chance is to reach the jeep!"

The vehicle was only about ten yards away, but it might have been a hundred. As they ran, the earth shook beneath their feet from the immense weight of the stampeding elephants.

Frank shot a quick glance over his shoulder. A three-ton bull elephant was bearing down on them, its ears spread wide, its eyes wild. Clouds of red dust created a choking crimson haze.

The distance between the boys and the herd

had narrowed rapidly by the time they reached the jeep. Joe vaulted into the driver's seat and switched on the ignition as Frank and Sammy tumbled over the sides. The old engine coughed, then died.

Joe's hand trembled. He turned the key again.

"Give it a little gas!" Frank shouted. "They're only a few feet away!"

With a rasping cough the engine turned over, and Joe floored the gas pedal. In the back of the jeep Frank felt the hot, stale breath of the lead elephant just as they shot forward.

Joe drove diagonally across the front of the herd, hoping to get clear. A line of trees and brush blocked his path. At the last moment he made a sharp left and drove parallel to the brush, keeping just a few yards ahead of the rampaging herd.

"There's a clearing just up ahead, on the right. We can make it!" Sammy shouted.

"We'd better!" Joe yelled back. "They'll be on us in another few seconds." He fought the wheel to maintain control as they bounced and pitched over the rocky terrain. Unexpectedly the jeep hit a large rock and lurched up on its side, nearly tossing the boys from the vehicle. Frank and Sammy gripped the roll bar.

Abruptly an opening appeared in the wall of the brush and trees. Without hesitating, Joe yanked the wheel to the right, sending the jeep into a two-wheel turn. The jeep made it through, but the turn was too sharp. The vehicle began to tip.

"Jump!" Joe warned.

He leapt into space, with Frank and Sammy only seconds behind him. They hit the ground and rolled out of the way of the crashing jeep. Metal shrieked and groaned as it flipped over several times and came to a crashing stop.

Frank whipped around in the direction of the elephants. The noisy, stampeding herd raced past them, not more than five yards away.

"You okay?" Joe asked, staggering over to Frank's side.

"Yeah," Frank replied, brushing the dust from his tattered clothes. "But for a minute there . . ."

Joe gripped his brother's shoulder. "I know what you mean. I didn't think we were going to make it, either."

Not far away Sammy picked himself up from the grass and brushed his clothes. He looked at the wrecked jeep, which now lay upside down and was covered in red dust.

"Dr. Bodine will not be happy," he said sadly.

Gingerly Joe touched his right side and winced with pain. There were several nasty cuts across his ribs.

"You'd better get that checked out," Frank advised.

"It's nothing," Joe insisted.

"Don't forget where we are," Frank warned. "If it gets infected, you'll be in bad shape."

"Okay, Mom," Joe teased. "I'll take care of it."

Just then Dr. Bodine, Oyamo, and Keesha drove up in the second jeep.

"Are you all right?" Oyamo shouted even before he stopped the vehicle. Dr. Bodine jumped down, a first-aid kit in her hands. Without hesitating, she began treating Joe's injuries with antiseptic.

Frank stared after the herd of elephants. Their flight was marked by a billowing cloud of reddish brown dust. Behind them, in the gathering dusk, he saw orange flames licking at the dry, brown grass. Billowing clouds of thick white smoke swirled over the plain, mixing with the dust from the stampede.

"The elephants are heading west toward the Tsavo Park!" Oyamo shouted to Dr. Bodine.

"Keep track of them and let me know where they stop," Rosalyn instructed.

After pressing gauze bandages across the cuts on Joe's chest, Rosalyn Bodine snapped the first-aid kit shut.

"We radioed the rangers about the brushfire," she told them. "They'll be here any minute now. If you two are up to it, we've got to get it under control. If it burns much longer, we could lose thousands of acres—and all the wildlife that live here."

"We're up to it, definitely," said Joe.

"Good, then. Let's go save some animals."

For the next hour the Hardys battled the brushfire alongside dozens of rangers who arrived in a convoy of jeeps and land cruisers. The fire spread fast. At first they had to beat down the flames with branches and shovels full of dirt. They dug ditches and cut down trees to create fire breaks.

It was early evening, and the African darkness began to fall quickly, without the lingering dusk that Frank and Joe were accustomed to. The smoke was thick, and Joe had tied his T-shirt around his face to protect his lungs. He thought it was hopeless until he saw Ranger Rawji arrive with a gas-powered pump on the back of a pickup. In no time a thick hose was thrown into the water hole and the fire fighters began to spray the flames. In minutes the fire was reduced to smoldering grass and charred trees.

By the time the last column of black smoke was extinguished, it was night. Frank and Joe gathered with the other fire fighters around the jeeps. Headlights and lanterns illuminated the site. Frank glanced around. Everyone looked exhausted, their faces and clothing soiled with soot and dirt. When he glanced down at his own clothes, he saw he was just as filthy.

Dr. Bodine stood on the back of one of the pickups and addressed the crowd.

"You've all done a terrific job," she said.

"I've radioed back to the compound, and my cooks have thrown together a big, hearty dinner for all of you."

The rangers cheered.

"Come to think of it, I haven't eaten since Mombasa," Joe said to Frank.

His brother laughed. "Well, you lasted this long—that's a major accomplishment."

They found a ride back to the compound in a ranger's jeep and gathered with the other fire fighters in the mess hall. The smell of dinner was mouthwatering, and Frank and Joe each grabbed a tray and lined up. With their plates heaped with savory meatballs, potatoes, and beans, they took their seats at a table beside Sammy. It wasn't long before the conversation turned to the brushfire.

"Well, at least the elephants got away safely," Joe remarked between mouthfuls of food. "Even if the fire burned a few acres of grassland."

"Yes, the elephants got away," Sammy said glumly. "But that was one of the only watering holes for miles, and this is the dry season. Now they will die of thirst."

Just then Oyamo came by with a tray of food and clambered over the bench to sit at their table.

"Ah, but the elephants are smarter than we are, I think," he said.

"What do you mean?" Joe asked.

"Dr. Bodine asked me to follow the herd, and I did. They went directly to another water hole, three miles south of the fire. We thought it was already dry, but it's not. So the elephants are safe. And they have water."

"They are safe for a while," Sammy commented, digging into his food. "Until the poachers find them."

Frank ate the rest of his dinner in almost complete silence. When he was finished he motioned to Joe and led his brother outside the mess hall.

"What's up, Frank?" Joe asked.

"I have an idea," Frank said. "There's a topographical map of the area on the wall in the front hall of the big house. I want to show you something."

Frank led Joe across the compound. "Remember what happened last night at the other water hole? The poachers ambushed the leopards when they came to drink. What if poachers started that fire to drive the elephants away?"

"You mean so they'd go to that other water hole that Oyamo mentioned?" Joe asked.

"Exactly," said Frank. "One that the rangers aren't watching."

They climbed the steps to the porch and entered the front hall of the house. The map was pinned to a large bulletin board just outside Dr. Bodine's office.

Frank put his finger on a spot that marked where the compound was and traced a line to the first water hole. It was marked on the map with a dotted circle.

"That's because it's dry part of the year," Frank explained. He traced an invisible line several inches below it to another small dotted circle. "That must be it. Three miles south, just like Oyamo said."

"And look!" Joe pointed to a broken line that curled across the map to the edge of the water hole. "According to the legend this is a dirt trail. If you're right, there could be a raid on those elephants tonight. But how do we get there?" Joe asked. "The dirt bikes were wiped out last night."

"Sammy?" Frank suggested. "He could get a jeep from the motor pool.

"One with a radio," Joe said. "So if we do run into poachers, we can call for help."

Frank and Joe left the main house and went back to the mess hall. The temperature had dropped, and the night felt almost cool to Joe. A sliver of moon had just risen above the tops of a row of palm trees.

At the mess hall Sammy was just finishing his dinner. The little Kenyan was exhausted, but after the Hardys explained their plan, he agreed to drive them.

They walked down the road to the garage and found a jeep. With Sammy at the wheel, the three of them slipped out of the compound.

Despite the waxing moon low in the sky, the

road was shrouded by a curtain of ebony blackness. The jeep's headlights illuminated only a thin path in front of them. They traveled for half an hour over a rutted dirt trail that led through a forest of shoulder-high scrub brush and tall grass. Frank was glad Sammy knew the way.

As they drew near the water hole, the still of the night was broken by the lethal staccato of automatic weapon fire.

"It's just over that hill!" Joe shouted over the roar of the jeep's engine.

"Cut the lights and take it slow," Frank cautioned Sammy. The driver obeyed, and the jeep plunged forward in almost total darkness. Halfway up the hill they heard engines start up and the sound of heavy trucks moving off.

"Hit it!" Frank told Sammy. Their driver floored the gas pedal, and the jeep leapt forward, racing up over the top of the hill.

From the crest Joe could see the distant lights of trucks racing across the plain in the opposite direction. Sammy turned on the lights of the jeep and drove down the hill to the edge of the water hole. The sight turned Joe's stomach.

Elephants, large and small, were sprawled on the ground, riddled with bullet holes. Some were dead. Others cried out in torment.

Joe felt a raging anger well up inside him. The gentle beasts had been butchered, their valuable ivory tusks hacked from their heads with chain saws and axes.

"Look there," Frank said, pointing at a smaller elephant. The white birthmark on the animal's forehead was unmistakable. Her chest heaved slowly, and blood streamed from her wounds.

"Rafiki," Frank whispered. As he reached her side, Rafiki let out a weak whimper. Her enormous brown eyes, brimming with pain, gazed up at him. He knelt beside her and carefully stroked her head. "I'm sorry, Rafiki," Frank said softly. "I'll find out who did this to you, and I'll get them for it."

Rafiki coiled her trunk and, with her last reserves of energy, dropped it across Frank's lap. She looked up at him once again, and her eyes closed. Then her chest stopped moving.

Rafiki was dead.

Chapter

11

FRANK KNELT OVER Rafiki's lifeless body.

"What can we do for the elephants?" Joe asked, his voice filled with rage and disbelief.

"Nothing," Frank said quietly. "Except get the people who did this."

The smell of death was all around them. In the distance they heard the eerie howls of jackals, scavengers of the dead, calling to their packs. A feast awaited.

"They'll be here soon," Frank said, rising and walking toward Joe. "We'd better get the rangers out here."

Sammy ran across the killing ground toward the two brothers. "I have radioed for the rangers," he told them.

"The poachers were driving off that way!"

Joe shouted, pointing east. "Let's go after them. At least we saw what direction they're heading!"

"They were headed up the other side of the valley," Sammy agreed. "If they clear the ridge, they will be lost to us. Let us follow them."

Sammy pushed the jeep as fast as he could across the treacherous terrain. It was hard going, especially in the dark. Loose rocks and potholes caught the wheels and slowed them down. By the time they reached the crest of the ridge on the other side of the valley, the poachers had vanished.

Joe slammed his fist against the side of the jeep. "We let'em get away."

"Take it easy, Joe," Frank told him. "They know this land and they're armed. Getting ourselves killed wouldn't do anyone any good."

"Let's get back to the elephants and wait for the rangers," Joe said.

An hour later the slaughter had been lit by kerosene lamps, flashlights, and vehicle headlights. Joe watched Rosalyn Bodine amid the carnage. Wind whipped her hair wildly about her face. Her clothes were stained red with blood.

"Dr. Bodine looks as if she's lost her family," Joe said as he and Frank walked with Ranger Rawji.

"Perhaps she has," the ranger said. "She has worked with these animals over fifteen years."

He rubbed his eyes wearily. "Before, there were a few attacks here and there. But now the criminals are tougher and more vicious. The poacher you captured yesterday refuses to give us any information. But somehow this killing will end!"

The next day the sky was cloudy but the temperature had climbed into the nineties by mid-morning. Because of the tragedy with the elephants and the late hours they had put in, Dr. Bodine had given Frank and Joe the day off.

After breakfast Frank retrieved Agent Lincoln's notebook from its hiding place. He and Joe stared at the strange words on the first page. One fascinated Joe.

"D—M—A—U," he spelled out loud. "I wonder . . ." he said, his voice trailing off.

"Wonder what?" Frank demanded.

Joe pointed at the word he had just spelled. "If you rearrange these letters it spells *duma*— Swahili for 'cheetah.' "

"Chris used Swahili words instead of English!" Frank exclaimed. "No wonder we weren't getting anywhere."

Joe grabbed his Swahili language guide. Together, the Hardys began unscrambling the words on the first page of the notebook.

"It's just a list of animal names in Swahili," said Frank. He was disappointed.

Joe stared at the notebook. They seemed so close to squeezing the notebook's secrets from the page. "Maybe Lincoln did something very simple with these Swahili words."

"Simple?" Frank asked, staring at the list of animal names. He circled the first letter in each word they had decoded.

O—L—D—M—A—S—A—I

Joe threw his fist into the air. "All right!"

Frank worked fast. In a few minutes the first page of the notebook revealed its secrets.

"Old Masai manya," he read aloud.

"Maybe it's an abbreviation for *manyatta*," Joe suggested.

"And the next words are Maktau Hills." Frank looked at his brother. "Sounds like a location."

"Of what?" Joe asked.

"The Masai *manyatta*," Frank suggested. "Maybe Tenga or Duncan can tell us if there's an old *manyatta* in the Maktau Hills." He grinned at Joe. "Let's ask Doc Bodine for the keys to a jeep."

Rosalyn Bodine was in her office, working at a desk strewn with papers. She looked weary from lack of sleep. Much to Frank's surprise, she granted his request to visit the Masai village without asking any questions.

"Is there a place around here called Maktau Hills?" Joe asked her.

Dr. Bodine nodded. "It's out past the Masai

manyatta. You don't want to go there, though. It's nothing but barren desert."

With that she turned back to her paperwork.

The Hardys picked up a jeep at the garage and headed for the *manyatta.* Frank pulled up in front of the village gate an hour later. Duncan greeted them warmly as they walked through the narrow opening. "What brings you here today?"

"We need to ask some questions about a friend of ours who is missing. The American named Chris Lincoln."

"Then you must talk to Tenga," Duncan told them. "They were friends."

The Hardys found Tenga on a hillside just outside the village, gazing off at the rolling hills that coasted to the horizon. The Masai teenager greeted them with enthusiasm. After a few words Frank asked Tenga about Maktau Hills.

Tenga nodded quickly and with a grin pointed toward the west. "Lincoln go there," he said. "I show you."

Grabbing binoculars from the jeep, the Hardys followed Tenga across grassy fields and up into the hills behind the village. For almost an hour they walked through brush and over rocks. Wild boars and gazelles grazed around them, barely noticing the human intruders. Finally they reached a tall pile of volcanic rock that overlooked a deep ravine. Below, Frank saw dusty trails leading into a barren region.

"Where do those trails go?" he asked.

"Maktau Hills," Tenga answered. "No life. Old *manyatta,* no people now."

Frank used his binoculars to scan the rocky hillside that led down into the ravine. Large boulders jutted up like jagged spikes. Suddenly Frank saw sunlight glint on something metal on a ledge ten feet below them.

"There's something down there!" he shouted at Joe. "Let's have a look."

The Hardys and Tenga scrambled down the steep incline until they stood on the narrow ledge.

"It's over there," Frank said, pointing toward the rocks where he had seen something shine. He walked over and knelt.

"What have you got?" Joe asked.

Frank held up a video camera. The camera was open. A water canteen lay a few feet away. "I hope this doesn't belong to anyone we know."

"It's Lincoln's!" Tenga exclaimed gleefully, holding up the video camera. "Lincoln's!"

Joe took the camera from Tenga. "It looks as if someone caught Lincoln shooting pictures and didn't like it."

"Exactly what I was thinking." Frank looked at the canteen. It was still half full of water. "I can't imagine him leaving his canteen behind, either. I keep hoping Lincoln is in hiding, or maybe being held prisoner. But the more we look, the more I think he's already dead."

They climbed back up to the top of the ravine. Walking farther along the edge, Frank saw a rutted trail zigzag down the steep side and out into the Maktau Hills.

"I want to get the jeep," said Frank. "Whatever Chris discovered is somewhere out there. I want to check on it."

The Hardys returned to the *manyatta* with Tenga. They thanked him and said goodbye before climbing into the jeep.

Frank took the wheel and drove back to the ravine. He followed the crude trail down the steep side until the ravine opened up into a broad, dusty plain, scattered with waist-high bushes. The land grew more and more barren as they drove farther. Finally Frank stopped the jeep, and they got out to look around.

"There have been a lot of animals passing through here," Joe said, pointing to the tracks.

"Look at this." Frank bent down to examine the dirt.

Joe walked over to his brother and knelt beside him. "Tire tracks. Heavy-duty ones."

"Probably from trucks," Frank added.

"These marks have to be recent," Joe said. "Between the wind and the animals, nothing would last more than a day or so out here."

Climbing back into the jeep, the Hardys followed the rough, dusty road, stopping periodically to check for tire tracks. In some places the ground was too hard for anything to leave a mark, but there was enough of a trail to lead them to the edge of a shallow, dry basin. Below them, half a mile away, was a large barn and several small huts around it.

"It looks deserted," said Frank, lowering his binoculars. "There doesn't seem to be anyone in sight for miles."

"This must be one of those abandoned *manyattas* Tenga mentioned," Joe said.

They drove down into the basin and stopped at the large barn. The nearby huts were made of mud and grass, but the barn had been built of weathered wood and roofed with corrugated tin. Several tiny windows had been boarded up on the inside. The stout wooden door, however, was in good shape and bolted with a squeaky padlock.

Frank went to the jeep and rummaged around for the tire iron. He jammed it into the loop of the padlock and twisted. The lock came apart easily.

Joe smiled. "It's lucky we're the good guys." He pushed the door open.

The Hardys were assaulted by a vile, rotting odor. Joe covered his nose with his hand.

"It smells like something died in there."

"Maybe a whole bunch of things," Frank replied soberly as he walked inside.

Three large wooden tables with stainless steel countertops stood in the middle of the barn. Each had run-off gutters that led to a single hole

over a pail. They were stained red. On one wall
bloodied leopard skins hung in rows.

On the other side of the barn were cages.
Sleeping animals and birds came to life as the
Hardys explored. There were two leopards, half
a dozen baboons, and dozens of colorful birds.

"They don't seem very healthy," Frank observed. "Otherwise they would have made a lot
of noise when we arrived."

"Look at this," Joe said. He moved to a desk
behind the door. It was covered with forms for
shipping cargo. All of them bore the same logo.

" 'Phoenix Enterprises,' " Frank read aloud.
"They're all blank except the part marked
'Destination Information.' "

"What does that say?" Frank asked.

Joe glanced over several of the forms. "Most
of them say Stockholm."

Frank took one to get a better look. "Stockholm, Sweden, appears to be where Phoenix is
also based. Look at the business address."

"And look at this." Joe held up a makeshift
ashtray. It was filled with brown cigarette stubs.
"Doesn't our man Rashid smoke this type of
cigarette?" he asked.

"He sure does. Look at these." Frank picked
up another pile of forms, and flipped through
them with his thumb. "Veterinary Health Certificates. Blank ones—except they've all been
signed by Dr. Bodine!"

He walked to the door and examined them

closer in the daylight. The signature was lighter than the rest of the document. It looked as if it had been photocopied onto the blank forms.

"They must trace over the signature to make it look genuine," he told Joe. "First they trick her into signing multiple copies of bogus forms. Then they use a photocopier to crank out as many as they need."

Frank put the forms back where he had found them. Enormous wooden crates were stacked at the far end of the barn. Joe found a crowbar and popped the lid on one of them.

"Ivory!" he exclaimed, gazing inside. Dozens of bloodied tusks had been packed in straw. "These were probably taken from the elephants they killed last night."

"Look over there," Frank called, motioning Joe behind a pile of stacked crates. They faced a wall of tools. Hanging from nails and shelving were hacksaws, machetes, and chain saws.

"This is what they used on Rafiki's herd."

"I say we get in touch with Dad and Jellicoe," Joe said. "They can stake this place out and nail these scuzzballs!"

Frank nodded. "Okay."

The Hardys went back outside and slipped the padlock back in place on the door.

"We still don't know who the major players are in this gang," Joe said. "I'm sure Rashid is involved, but who at the compound?"

"Maybe Dad'll have some ideas," Frank said as he climbed into the jeep.

Joe opened the door on the passenger side. "I'd say we did a good day's work—"

Without warning Joe stiffened, and his eyes became fixed and staring. His hand flew to his neck, where he pulled a small dart from his skin. A tranquilizer dart. He felt a burning sensation where the dart had hit him.

"Frank," he gasped, "I've been shot." Before he could utter another word, Joe's eyes rolled up into his head, and he crumpled to the ground.

Frank rose from his seat, just as he felt something sharp pierce the skin between his shoulder blades. He reached back and felt a thin metal cylinder embedded in his skin. Whatever was in the dart was acting fast. His head felt light, and the world began to swim before his eyes. He swooned in his seat, trying desperately to stay conscious. He couldn't move.

"Joe," Frank murmured. Daylight faded. He felt as if he were falling into a dark pit.

Chapter

12

FRANK HARDY couldn't move. He tried to lift his hands and shift his legs, but they were sluggish and heavy. He couldn't even open his eyes. He took a deep breath and began to gag and cough. His mouth filled with dust. Concentrating hard, he forced himself to open his eyes. A painful glare almost blinded him, but slowly his vision cleared.

He was lying on his side, with his head slumped on the ground. Before him, as far as he could see, was nothing but a vast, flat wasteland of dust and shrubs. Gnarled, dead trees lay like bleached bones strewn across a cemetery. His shirt and shoes were missing.

He vaguely remembered the deserted *manyatta*, the darts, losing consciousness. The poachers must have come back. They had shot him and Joe with tranquilizer guns.

Somewhere behind him, Frank heard a moan. He rolled in the direction of the sound and spotted Joe lying a few feet away, facedown. His shirt and shoes were missing, too.

"Wake up," Frank croaked, crawling toward his brother.

Joe managed to lift his head and look around. "Where—?" His question was choked off by the dryness in his throat. He swallowed, trying to get some saliva to flow.

"Near as I can tell," Frank said, "we're in the middle of nowhere."

"Oh, good," Joe replied. He pushed himself up, wincing from the aches in every joint of his body. "I was afraid we were lost."

Slowly Frank and Joe rose to their feet.

"Judging from the position of the sun," Joe said, "I'd bet it's about ten or eleven in the morning. We must have been unconscious all night."

Frank shook his head, trying to clear his thoughts. "Someone should be out looking for us by now." He gazed up at the sky. "We're facing east, which is the direction of the compound."

"How do you know the compound isn't behind us somewhere?"

Frank pointed off to their right. Far in the distance Joe could just make out the snow-covered peak of Mount Kilimanjaro. "I remember seeing it on the map in Dr. Bodine's office. It was west of the compound."

"So, what are we waiting for?" Joe asked.

Frank mustered a smile. "A taxi?"

"Funny." Joe stretched his arms to ease out the kinks in his muscles. "Let's start walking."

Fighting off waves of dizziness and pressing thirst, Frank and Joe trekked slowly east across the barren plains. The ground was parched and pitted with sharp rocks and stones.

The sun was their greatest enemy, though. Its relentless dry heat evaporated the moisture from their bodies, cooking their bare flesh.

"This is a rotten way to get a tan," Joe muttered hoarsely.

"I'll complain to our travel agent," Frank retorted.

They struggled on for another hour until they came upon the skeleton of a deer or antelope. Its head had been dragged several feet from the body.

"Vultures?" Joe said, pointing at the remains.

Frank was looking up at the sky. "They'll do it to us, too, if they get half a chance.

Joe followed Frank's gaze and saw two of the great black birds circling overhead. "We're not supposed to make it out of this one, are we?"

"That's what the poachers intended," Frank said. "Look, we can't be too far from help. We've just got to keep moving."

The Hardys traveled in silence for a while. The harsh African sun beat down on them, draining their strength and burning their fair skin. It was obvious to Frank that death was common in this desert land. Bleached bones and skulls were scattered everywhere, the final remains of wildebeest, gazelles, and other creatures that had lost their fight to survive.

"Wait!" Joe called to Frank. His voice was raspy, and he was starting to lag behind. He dropped down to the ground and examined his feet.

"Are you hurting?" Frank asked, kneeling beside his brother.

"You could say that," Joe replied. "My feet are burning from the heat of the ground."

"Mine, too," Frank said, examining his own feet. "Got any ideas?"

Joe thought for a moment. "Yeah," he said. He picked up a sharp piece of rock and used it to rip off part of his pant leg. Then he tied the fabric around his foot. He repeated the steps for the other foot. "That should work."

Frank grabbed the rock and followed Joe's example. Once more they set out across the desert, making faster progress with their protected feet.

The heat continued to beat down on them. I have to take my mind off it, Joe thought to himself. He began to play a word game. "*Jambo* means 'hello,'" he mumbled. "*Kwaheri* means 'goodbye.' *Punda* is 'zebra,' *simba* is 'lion,' *duma* is 'cheetah.' ''

For quite some time Joe tried to remember all the Swahili words he had learned, the greetings, the questions, the names of animals and everyday objects. This helped until he found the jackal hole.

It was about two feet in diameter, burrowed into clay on the side of a low hill. He didn't know how deep, and he didn't want to look.

Bones were scattered around the entrance. Some of them were unmistakably human.

"Frank!" Joe screamed. He staggered backward and tripped over something. It was a red knapsack, torn and empty. He grabbed it and jumped to his feet, almost colliding with Frank. Joe pointed to the jackal's hole.

"Jackals don't kill," Frank said. "They scavenge from the dead. The jackal probably dragged the body back to its lair."

"Check this out," Joe said, handing him the faded red knapsack. On the back Chris Lincoln's name was written with felt-tip marker, along with a New York address.

"Poor guy," Joe said. "The jackals didn't drag him here. He was dumped. By his murderers."

Frank nodded toward the bones. "There's nothing we can do for Lincoln now except keep going. Let's leave the knapsack here. Someone's got to come to retrieve these bones anyway, and we're too exhausted to carry it."

They hid the knapsack in the branches of a leafless shrub. Then they walked for another hour, watching the sun climb slowly toward noon. Joe felt his fair skin burning. His mouth was dry, and his tongue felt like a cotton ball. His head started swimming, and he tried to steady himself against the impossible tilt of the earth.

Frank saw his brother teetering. He staggered to Joe's side, grabbed him under the arms, and steadied him against his side.

Joe felt Frank's reassuring arms and took a deep breath. His head began to clear. He pushed on, leaning on Frank for support.

They walked as far as they could before Joe finally slid to the ground, exhausted. He lay there with his eyes shut, wanting to say something, to crack a joke to break the silence, but his mouth was dry and his mind refused to work. Anyway, their situation wasn't funny, he told himself. There was no relief in sight, not even shade to shelter them until it was dark and cooler.

Weak from thirst and the heat, Frank glanced at the sun and estimated that it was early afternoon. He peered through the shimmering heat waves dancing on the barren land and blinked to clear a mirage. But when he opened his eyes, it was still there, so far in the distance that it was barely a hazy spot of color.

"Trees! Bushes!" he cried. "Joe!" Frank

dropped to the ground and shook his brother. "We have to keep going!"

Joe heard his brother shouting. He wanted to sleep, to go away from the heat and the pain and the thirst. He heard his brother shout his name again and struggled to open his eyes.

"There's water over there," Frank told him.

"How far?" Joe asked, his voice a rattle.

"I don't know how far, but I can see trees." Frank grabbed Joe, dragging him to his feet. "At least we'll have some shade," he muttered, taking Joe's weight against his shoulder once again.

All they found when they got there was a patch of thick mud surrounded by scrawny bushes.

"We can use the mud to cool our skin," Frank said, digging a handful out and splashing it over his sunburned shoulders. It felt like cool water. Joe dug up a handful, and when Frank looked up, Joe splashed it against his face. Frank hit Joe with a handful, and for a moment they were lost in a mudfight. But only for a moment. There was still no water.

"Look!" Joe pointed a mud-smeared arm at the wet earth. Water was percolating into the gouges they had made in the mud.

Frank put his hand in one of the tiny puddles, and then sniffed suspiciously at his wet fingers. "Smells like water." He nodded. He put his fingers in his mouth. It tasted clean, if a little gritty.

Joe knelt down and scooped up a handful. He

sipped at it. To his parched mouth it tasted like a cool mountain stream.

Then he heard the growl.

"A lion," Frank gasped. He stared into the bushes surrounding the mud patch and spotted a tawny shape running between some low, leafless trees.

"Steady," Joe whispered. "He might just be curious."

The beast snarled and began to move toward them. It was definitely a lion, with a mane ringing its massive face. It stopped at the perimeter of the bush and stared, scratching at the ground with an immense paw.

Frank glanced quickly around and spotted a gnarled old tree with a trunk that forked about six feet off the ground. It was at least thirty feet away.

"The tree!" Frank shouted. "Run for it! Now!"

He grabbed Joe and pushed him. They raced toward the tree. The lion gave a long roar and began to sprint beside the mud patch. When they reached the tree, the lion roared again and charged. Frank boosted Joe up onto the lowest limb.

Joe grabbed a tree branch and reached back for Frank. "Give me your hand!" he shouted. Frank scrambled desperately up the slippery tree trunk.

Joe watched in horror as the lion pounced toward Frank, its deadly claws extended.

Chapter

13

FRANK CLUNG TO the trunk and saw the claws, the teeth, the flashing eyes. He saw no way out.

Suddenly a figure leapt from the bushes to his left. It was a man with skin as dark as charcoal, glistening with oil and sweat, wearing Masai beads and a loincloth. He ran in front of the charging lion and crouched defiantly, his long spear pointed at the beast. He pushed the other end against the soft earth to anchor it. In his other hand he held a leather shield.

Frank couldn't believe what happened next. The Masai screamed and charged the lion, his spear impaling the beast. The lion went limp, dragging both of them to the ground. Quick and agile, the man rolled free, pulling a long-handled knife from his belt and gripping it tightly. The lion didn't move. It was already dead.

The Masai looked at Frank, then at Joe perched on his branch still. His expression was both stunned and exhilarated.

"Tenga!" Frank exclaimed. His legs and arms buckled, and he lost consciousness and slid from the trunk.

Joe scrambled down from the tree and knelt beside Frank, cradling his head. Tenga poured a slender stream of water from a leather canteen onto Frank's mouth. Joe saw Frank's eyes flutter and open. Tenga pulled the canteen away.

"Thanks," Frank said weakly, resting his head back.

"Rest." Tenga gave the canteen to Joe. "I will return."

He wrested his spear from the body of the lion. Then he turned to Frank and Joe, waving it in the air in a gesture of victory. He shouted something at Frank in his own language and disappeared into the bushes.

"You okay, Joe?" Frank asked.

Joe nodded. "Thanks to you. But don't you ever do that for me again."

Frank nodded and closed his eyes. "I'll make a note." He wanted to say something else, but he suddenly felt very tired. Then he didn't feel anything at all.

When Frank awoke, he was lying on a bed of cowhides inside a Masai hut. Ranger Pope Rawji was leaning over him, applying a damp cloth to his forehead. Joe lay next to him, watching.

Frank found it hard to say anything until Rawji handed him a glass of water.

"How long have we been here?" he asked.

"A couple of hours," Joe replied. "I just came to myself. We're at the *manyatta*. In Tenga's hut."

As if on cue, the young Masai entered the hut. "You are okay?" he asked, nodding his own head in the obvious hope that they were.

Joe laughed and remembered a Swahili saying from the guidebook. *"Habari sana.* All is good."

"You can say that again," Frank said. His brother's long hours with his Swahili guidebook were obviously paying off. Singing and cheering sounds came from outside the hut.

"They are celebrating something," Pope Rawji explained before Frank or Joe even asked. There was a proud look in his eye.

"Tenga's lion. He passed his rite of manhood," Frank said. "He has become a warrior."

Pope smiled. "Of course, as a ranger, I know nothing of this, because it would be illegal. But let us say that he killed the lion to save your life. His people have chosen to celebrate that."

Frank could see the pride in Tenga's face. The law versus thousands of years of tradition.

Frank turned to Rawji. "Before he left to get help, Tenga said something to me in the Masai language. Could you ask him what it was?"

The ranger questioned Tenga, who replied with a mischievous glint in his brown eyes. Ranger Rawji grinned.

"He told you that today was his day for the lion. Someday, Frank Hardy, you will have to find your own."

Frank took Tenga's hand and shook it. "Thanks, my friend."

Outside the hut children's voices chanted for Tenga to come out. He waved and left through the low door, letting a cowhide curtain fall behind him.

"Half the police force in the country has been looking for you," Rawji told the Hardys. "When you didn't return to the compound yesterday, Dr. Bodine telephoned me right away. Apparently you two have been a little accident prone ever since you arrived."

He looked at Frank and Joe as if he expected them to start explaining. Instead of waiting, however, he continued. "We found your jeep last night, not far from here. Tenga told me how you found Lincoln's camera and the canteen. What happened after that?"

"Can we have a moment alone?" Joe asked the ranger, glancing quickly at Frank.

Rawji nodded slowly. "Sure," he said somewhat reluctantly, and then left the hut.

"We've got to trust someone," Joe said, turning to Frank. "Look, right now the poachers think we're dead. With the ranger's help we can set a trap that might net everybody.''

"Just to be safe," Frank cautioned, "we don't say anything about Dad's cover until we've talked to him.''

Frank and Joe called Ranger Rawji back in and told him that they were searching for Chris Lincoln—and how it had got them stranded in the desert. Then they reached the part about the jackal's lair and what they had seen there.

"So we must assume it is Mr. Lincoln that you found." The ranger paused for a moment. "And you say the poachers' hideout is in the abandoned *manyatta* in the Maktau Hills?"

"Right," said Joe. "Does anyone know that we're alive other than you and the Masai?"

"No," Rawji replied. "Not even Dr. Bodine. And she has been calling constantly.''

Frank leaned toward the ranger. "Then if you'll let us make a phone call, I think we can pull this whole thing together.''

Pope's eyes narrowed. "These people have committed horrible crimes against my country. I want to see them pay dearly. I will drive you back to the compound and you can make your telephone call.''

It was almost evening by the time the Hardys reached the Bodine Animal Research Compound. The sun was low in the west. Frank and Joe found the big house empty. Dr. Bodine wasn't

132

in her office. In the garage Sammy was tuning up a Land-Rover.

"Dr. Bodine left with Oyamo and Keesha," he told them. "To search for you, Frank and Joe."

"Where?" Joe asked.

Sammy shrugged.

Frank and Joe went back to Dr. Bodine's office, and Frank dialed the contact number in Mombasa that their father had given them. A few minutes later Fenton Hardy was on the line.

Frank quickly filled him in on the events of the last two days.

"You really trust your contact there?" Fenton asked.

"You mean Ranger Rawji?" Frank asked. "Yes, Dad. We do."

"All right, then," said Fenton. "It's all going to come down tonight, and we could use his help. I've lined up a meeting with the poachers for midnight tonight. They want to sell me some ivory. We're meeting at the Phoenix warehouse at the Dhow Docks in Mombasa."

"What do you want us to do?" Frank asked.

"The poachers will try to move that ivory as soon as possible. I want you to stake out the poachers' hideout in the Maktau Hills right away with Ranger Rawji. Don't try to stop them. With their automatic rifles, they're too dangerous. As soon as they load the trucks, contact Agent Jellicoe at that number I gave you. He'll let me know the contrabrand is on its way."

"Jellicoe!" Frank said with surprise. "You contacted him finally?"

"He's here in Mombasa," Fenton said. "He'll be working with the local police to back me up. The police will arrest the smugglers at this end."

"Sounds like a plan," Frank said slowly. "Are you sure you don't want us for backup, too?"

"Don't worry about me," Fenton reassured his son. "Just take care of your own end."

"I don't like the part about you going in alone," Frank told him. "Even if you are working undercover as a buyer of ivory."

Fenton tried to reassure Frank. "I've done this kind of thing before, Frank. Before you were born."

Frank smiled. "See you at the finish line."

"As always"—Fenton paused—"you boys be careful."

"As always." Frank said goodbye, and hung up the phone. He turned to Joe. "Dad wants us to stake out the poachers' hideout tonight with Ranger Rawji. When they move the ivory, he'll get the authorities to bust them in Mombasa."

"Great!" Joe exclaimed. "Finally these guys will be nailed."

The phone rang. Frank picked it up. It was Jellicoe.

"Your famous father finally contacted me," Jellicoe said. "He's in Mombasa."

"I was just talking to him," Frank told the

customs agent. Frank gently told him of Lincoln's death.

Jellicoe didn't seem to take the news of Chris Lincoln's death well. Frank heard him bang his fist against a metal desk. "You're sure it was Chris's body?"

"I'm sorry," Frank said. "It's rough when your partner is killed. Of course, we couldn't positively identify the remains, but the knapsack had his name on it."

"You and your brother have done a great job, Frank," Jellicoe said. "I just want to get these killers and put them out of business."

"Are you sure you don't need some more backup in Mombasa?" Frank asked. He still felt uncomfortable about Fenton Hardy going into the poachers' lair completely alone.

"The Mombasa police will be there ready and waiting," Jellicoe told him. "I'll be there, too, along with some other agents. You and Joe just take care of things out at Maktau Hills and let us know when they move out."

Frank slowly put the telephone back in its cradle and turned to Joe. Everything was falling into place, and yet he couldn't shake the feeling that something was seriously wrong.

"Let's talk to Ranger Rawji," Frank said. "We only have a few hours to get everything ready."

Rawji was waiting on the porch outside the big house. Frank filled him in on what was happening in Mombasa. Rawji was delighted.

"Now we will stop these savages," he proclaimed, pounding his fist into the palm of his other hand.

They went down the steps and climbed into Rawji's jeep. Rawji put it in gear and drove out the gates of the compound. The muted colors of the brief African twilight hid the trail of dust that blew up from the jeep's wheels, and as long as a glimmer of sunset remained in the west, they were able to drive without headlights.

Just as night fell, they arrived at the edge of the shallow basin where the abandoned *manyatta* was. A quarter moon had just risen, casting a low silver light over the barren land. Half a mile below them the barn was well lit, and several vehicles were parked out front. They watched men loading birdcages into a van.

"That's weird," said Frank. "They're using a pretty small truck."

"It's less conspicuous?" Joe suggested.

"Maybe," said Frank. "But it can't hold all the crates of ivory we saw."

"That's right." Joe agreed. "I wonder what's going on down there."

Suddenly Frank heard the sound of a gun bolt being thrown behind them.

"Why don't you go down and find out?" said an unmistakable, heavily accented voice.

It was Rashid.

Chapter

14

FRANK, JOE, and Ranger Rawji turned.

Rashid was standing behind them, pointing an automatic rifle. Behind him stood two other men in dark clothes. Both carried automatic weapons. Rashid nodded at one of them and then jerked his head toward the ranger.

The henchman stepped forward, moving behind Ranger Rawji. He smashed the barrel of his rifle into the ranger's head. Rawji collapsed like a rag doll, blood spouting from his wound.

"He is useful to us alive and unconscious," Rashid said, playing a flashlight over Rawji's slumped form. He looked up at the Hardys. "You are not useful to us alive at all. Let's go." With his rifle he gestured them toward the barn.

All the way down the hill Frank wondered

what had gone wrong. Somehow, the poachers had been one step ahead of them ever since they had arrived in Kenya. But Rashid's ambush was nothing compared to the shock that met the Hardys eyes when they entered the barn.

Standing by one of the tables was Rosalyn Bodine. Her eyes grew wide when she saw Frank and Joe. She was clearly terrified.

"How did—?" she started.

"Be quiet!" her guard ordered. It was the man who had posed as a peddler in Mombasa when the Hardys were abducted. He grinned wickedly. Oyamo and Keesha lay on the floor beside a crate, their hands tied and their mouths taped. Oyamo was unconscious, his face bloodied.

"It seems that Dr. Bodine and her friends came looking for you," Rashid told the Hardys. He pushed Joe across the room. "It was a mistake for them. And we do not have much time."

Frank noticed that most of the crates and cages were gone. "You moved things out already!"

"We had to," said Rashid. "When the boss told us you were coming, we had to change plans."

Frank and Joe looked at each other. Someone had betrayed them by revealing their plans to the smuggler. But who was it?

"So a higher-up is giving you orders," Frank said defiantly. "When we bust your ring, Rashid, we'll keep looking until we find out who it is."

The swarthy smuggler laughed in their faces. "The information will do you little good now."

The fake peddler and another henchman pushed Frank and Joe to the floor and tied their hands and feet. When they were finished, they began roping Dr. Bodine to a post near the door.

Rashid leered at his prisoners. "You have all been a great deal of trouble." Then he looked directly at Frank and Joe. "Especially you two. Like Chris Lincoln, you poked your noses in too many places. Now we are forced to close down our operation here. But first we will tie up a few loose ends. And this time you won't escape."

"Escape what?" Frank asked.

"Gasoline," said Joe. The odor of fuel pervaded the barn. Two of Rashid's henchmen were sprinkling it all over the room. They worked quickly and tossed the gas cans aside.

Rashid struck a match while the other thugs headed for the barn's exit. He watched it flare up and, with a final, leering smile, threw it into a pool of gasoline. Instantly the flames shot along the floor, encircling the crates and creeping up the walls.

"I'm afraid it will be unpleasant," said Rashid. "But don't worry. It won't take long." He stepped outside and shut the door tightly.

Lying on his side against a crate, Frank watched the flames race across the floor, consuming tables, boxes, chairs, and anything else in their path. He heard engines start up outside, and then the sound of the poachers driving off. Smoke and noxious fumes burned his lungs, forcing him to cough. Overhead the corrugated-tin roof creaked and buckled. Frank knew that at any moment it would collapse.

He turned toward the others. Oyamo lay unconscious on the floor, blood staining his shirtsleeve. Beside him Keesha struggled against the ropes that held her. She was unable to speak because of the tape across her mouth, but her eyes showed her hysteria.

Across the room Rosalyn pulled at the ropes that bound her to the post. "It's no good," she called. "They're too tight." The flames were closing in on her fast. It was obvious to Frank that Dr. Bodine was in serious trouble.

Suddenly Joe cried out, "I've got an idea! Look over there." Joe gestured with his head through the mounting flames to the back wall. The poachers had stored their tools there. But a line of flames separated him from them.

"How are you going to get there?" Frank shouted over the roar of the fast-moving flames.

Joe coughed. The smoke was getting thicker. He kept his head close to the floor where the air was clearer and sized up a stack of wooden crates nearby. There were three of them, one in front and two behind, piled on top of each other.

With his hands and feet tied it was difficult to keep his balance, but slowly Joe pushed himself to his feet. With the heavy smoke stinging his eyes, he hopped forward, leaping onto the first box, standing again, and pulling himself up on top of the second.

He was in luck. The poachers had abandoned their tools and saws.

Flames licked at his heels. Joe jumped down on the other side of the crates, his body slamming into the wall as he knocked tools in all directions. Pain lanced through his shoulder, but he scarcely noticed it. His eyes lit up when he saw a machete on the floor.

Joe tottered and fell, took a breath of the cooler air close to the ground, and turned his back against the machete's blade. He angled the sharp edge against his ropes and began sawing. The blade sliced into his fingers, then his wrist as he worked the rope up and down.

Joe gritted his teeth against the pain. He could feel his blood, sticky and hot, seeping from cuts in his wrists. "Come on, come on!" he urged.

Suddenly the rope gave. His hands were free! Joe rolled over and grabbed the machete by the handle, quickly slashing the ropes that bound his feet.

The flames around Rosalyn Bodine were closing fast, and she was almost overcome by the thick smoke. Joe ran through the burning barn to reach her.

With a quick slashing motion, Joe cut her free from the post. Dr. Bodine fell forward to her knees, taking a quick breath of air near the floor.

"Thanks," she panted. She added with a grim smile, "But what kept you?"

"Caught in traffic," Joe shot back.

The flames had completely encircled Frank, Keesha, and Oyamo, separating them from Joe and Dr. Bodine. Joe spotted the stainless-steel countertop.

"Help me knock this over!" he shouted at Rosalyn Bodine.

The metal was too hot to touch with their bare hands. Placing the soles of their boots against it, they tipped the heavy table over. The steel clattered against the floor, extinguishing some of the flames. The long metal surface made a perfect bridge through the fire.

Joe rushed across it and cut the others free. Frank picked up Oyamo and slung him over his shoulders as Joe grabbed Keesha. The young woman had almost passed out from the choking fumes.

Rosalyn Bodine tore off her jacket and beat the flames away from the door. Joe swung the machete hard against the lock, shattering it. He kicked the door open.

They ran from the building just as the roof caved in with a loud crash. Flames and sparks rained down around them. As they ran toward the road, Ranger Rawji came stumbling down the hill.

"You are safe!" he cried out. "Thank goodness." There was a nasty gash across his right

142

temple, and dark red blood stained his neck and shirt.

Frank turned to Dr. Bodine, who stood beside Oyamo's unconscious body, cutting Keesha's bonds.

"So why'd they go through the trouble of trying to bump off you three?" he asked the veterinarian.

"Because we were desperate to find you two when you didn't come back to the compound," Dr. Bodine told him. "I remembered your asking about Maktau Hills before you went to the Masai village. We drove out here to look for you. Instead we stumbled on a convoy of trucks leaving this abandoned *manyatta*."

"That must have been when they moved the ivory out," Frank said.

"Probably, although we never saw what was in the trucks," Rosalyn told them. "They quickly took us prisoner."

"They had another reason for wanting you dead, though," Joe told the veterinarian.

Dr. Bodine looked at him strangely.

"They've used your signature on veterinary health certificates to help them smuggle animals out of the country," Joe explained.

Dr. Bodine was obviously stunned. "That's impossible!"

Joe shook his head. "I saw them myself." Quickly he told her about the multiple copies of the certificates he had seen on Rashid's clipboard at the dock in Mombasa. Then he pointed to the barn, which was now a raging inferno. "Then Rashid and Phoenix Enterprises photocopied your signature onto blank certificates. We saw them in the barn."

Orange firelight flickered across Dr. Bodine's dust-streaked face. "What a fool I've been," she said.

"Look," Joe said. "This is a slick bunch of criminals we're dealing with. They'll stop at nothing. It could have happened to anyone."

Nearby, Keesha cradled Oyamo's head in her arms. She looked up at the Hardys. Oyamo moaned softly. Dr. Bodine strode over to them, knelt, and felt his pulse.

"He tried to fight back, and they knocked him unconscious," Rosalyn explained to Frank and Joe. "He needs treatment quickly. We've got to get him back to the compound."

Suddenly a knot twisted in Frank's stomach.

Joe saw his brother blanch. "What's the matter, Frank?"

"I just figured out what's been bothering me since we left the compound. It's Jellicoe."

Joe was puzzled. "What do you mean, it's Jellicoe?"

"Just before I hung up, I asked if he needed some backup help in Mombasa when Dad went to meet the poachers. Jellicoe said, just take care of things in the Maktau Hills."

Joe didn't like where this was leading. "Go on."

"I never told Jellicoe the hideout was in the Maktau Hills! I'm positive I didn't mention it."

Joe felt the blood in his body run cold. "He's the only one who's been aware of all our moves!"

"And Chris Lincoln's," Frank pointed out. "Lincoln gave all his information to Jellicoe, and when he started closing in on the poachers, Jellicoe got rid of him. Then he must have searched Lincoln's hut at the Masai village. I found partly smoked cigarettes there—and Jellicoe only takes a couple of puffs before putting his cigarettes out."

"He's one of them!" Joe said, horrified. "He's a poacher!"

Frank nodded. "That's how our cover was blown when we were kidnapped in Mombasa. And I bet Jellicoe had something to do with that puff adder as well. He wanted us out of the way, either by scaring us—or worse."

Joe grabbed his brother's arm. "Frank, if Jellicoe knows everything, we've got to warn Dad! He's walking into a trap!"

Chapter

15

FRANK SPOTTED Dr. Bodine's jeep parked near one of the huts. "We have to get to Mombasa," he told her. "Our father's life is at stake."

"It's all yours," she said, motioning toward the jeep. "We'll go with Ranger Rawji."

Frank and Joe carried Oyamo and placed him in the backseat of the ranger's Land-Rover. Rosalyn and Keesha piled into the front.

"When we reach the compound, I will contact the Mombasa police and send them to the Phoenix warehouse," Rawji told Frank. Quickly he gave them directions to a highway four miles across the barren land. "Good luck," he said.

Frank and Joe jumped into the jeep and raced down the rutted track that led across the barren land. The quarter moon gave them just enough illumination to see where they were going. Dust billowed and swirled around the speeding jeep. Finally Joe steered onto a paved highway. They turned east, toward the coast.

"Step on it, Joe, please! Gun it!" Frank shouted.

Joe floored the accelerator, and the engine almost screamed in protest. The jeep bounced over the blacktop, picking up speed.

For a long time Frank stared at the open highway, thinking of the danger they were in. If Jellicoe really was one of the poachers, and they didn't get there in time to warn their father, he was a dead man.

Fifteen minutes later they roared across the Makupa Causeway and down Jomo Kenyatta Avenue. The streets were empty. Frank glanced at his watch. It was 11:55 P.M. In five minutes their father would be walking into the trap.

Joe whipped through the Old Town. "There are the docks!" he shouted.

"Let's ditch the jeep here," Frank said.

Joe parked on the street. The Hardys jumped out and quietly crept along the wharf. The streetlights were dim and cast long dark shadows. Frank pressed against the facade of one of the warehouses that lined the wharf.

"Stick to the shadows for cover," he whispered.

Joe nodded. Silently he pointed ahead. The Phoenix warehouse was at the end of the wharf.

There was no sign of any movement. They heard water lapping gently at the pylons that supported the old wharf. Staying close together, the Hardys moved forward until they were at the warehouse next to the Phoenix one. Suddenly, behind them, a door creaked open on rusty hinges. Frank and Joe whirled around.

It was Jellicoe.

The rogue customs agent held a .44 magnum in his hand, and a half-smoked cigarette dangled from his mouth. "If you two are here, then things went seriously wrong out at Maktau Hills."

"You've been behind this all along," Frank snarled. "Everything the authorities planned, the poachers knew about because you passed on the information to them."

Jellicoe gave a little laugh, the cigarette bobbing between his lips. "Just a matter of playing both sides against the middle," he said.

"Did that include murdering Chris Lincoln and dumping his body in the desert for the jackals to eat?" Frank demanded.

Jellicoe curled his lip and sneered. "Let's just say Lincoln found out too much. He said he kept a notebook, but I never did find it. It doesn't matter now." He took out his cigarette and crushed it on the floor with his foot.

"And you're the one who put that snake in Frank's bed, aren't you?" Joe said.

Jellicoe nodded. "Yeah, that was me. I figured

I'd kill one of you and the other one would take a hint and take a hike. But you two don't listen. Too bad.''

Another man stepped out of the warehouse. It was the man who had held them at gunpoint in the truck when the Hardys were abducted. This time he carried a long knife with a sharp, shiny blade. Jellicoe motioned Frank and Joe inside the nearby warehouse.

Reluctantly they walked in. Jellicoe and his associate followed and closed the door. A small window looked across fifty feet of water to the Phoenix wharf.

"The longer you boys stayed, the more I realized you were trouble." Jellicoe shook his head. "Such a sweet racket we had here, smuggling animals, exotic birds, ivory, leopard skins. We made a bundle at it. And now—"

"The police are onto you," Joe said, gritting his teeth. He could barely restrain an urge to throw himself on Jellicoe, despite the gun pointed at him.

"Maybe, maybe not," Jellicoe said calmly. "Either way I'm going to get rid of you guys and your father—once and for all. Then I'm out of here. To Stockholm. The boss and I have enough stashed away to live high on the hog."

Joe exchanged a knowing glance with Frank when Jellicoe mentioned a boss. Someone else was in charge of this operation, and they didn't know that person's identity.

"How could you do this?" Frank asked, stalling for time. "You not only turned against the agency, but you set up your own partner."

"I tried to cut Lincoln in when he found out about me, but he said no. He was going to do the right thing." Jellicoe shrugged. "It was nothing personal. Nothing personal against you boys, either. Strictly business."

Just then Joe and Frank heard a car engine. Frank glanced out the dusty window. The car was heading along the Phoenix wharf.

"That'll be your father," Jellicoe said. "I'll wait to make sure he's taken care of. Then I'll deal with you."

"What makes you think your trap will work?" Joe sneered. "The police are on the way and—"

"I don't care how fast the police get here, kid. Your old man can't punch out a bomb." Jellicoe started laughing.

Joe lost it. "Dad!" he screamed, diving toward the window.

Jellicoe aimed his gun and squeezed the trigger. Frank's foot came up, and connected with Jellicoe's wrist. The gun misfired, and the bullet hit the ceiling. The magnum flew from the agent's hand.

Jellicoe roared with rage. He started toward Frank. He was bigger and heavier than the younger man, but Frank didn't hold back. He whirled on one foot and served a lightning-fast roundhouse kick to Jellicoe's jaw. The customs agent slammed back against a wall of crates, blood streaming from his mouth. He slumped to the floor, jerked, and was still.

The other man ran at Frank, ready to drive his long shiny dagger into his back.

Joe Hardy jumped, tackling the man around his knees and knocking him over. The knife skittered across the floor. Instantly Joe was on top of him. He clenched his fist and slammed his attacker in the side of his head. The man's eyes rolled upward and shut.

Without a word the two brothers raced through the door and onto the wharf. Their father's car was parked in front of Phoenix Enterprises. No one was in it.

"Dad!" Joe shouted.

The Hardys bolted down the Phoenix dock.

"Get out, Dad!" Frank screamed as loud as he could. "It's a trap! There's a bomb!"

The explosion was deafening. Joe flew backward, a terrible pain in his ears. He hit the ground with Frank rolling on top of him. The brothers pulled their bodies together in a ball as broken glass and jagged wood showered down around them. Columns of fire erupted through the shattered roof of the Phoenix warehouse, and flames instantly engulfed the building.

When the deadly rain of debris stopped, Joe pushed Frank away and staggered up. Somewhere in the African night, police sirens were screaming and coming closer. Firelight flickered across Joe's shocked face as he stared at the inferno.

Slowly Frank rose to his feet. He screamed his father's name.

The only answer was the thunderous roar of the burning building. Despite the fire's heat, he felt a cold chill just beneath his skin.

A moment later police cars raced up the pier, sirens screaming and red lights flashing.

A stocky man wearing a police officer's uniform stood in front of the two brothers.

"Frank and Joe Hardy?" he asked.

Frank nodded without taking his eyes off the burning building.

"Ranger Rawji telephoned from the Bodine Animal Research Compound," the policeman said. "He suggested we might make some arrests here. A matter involving poachers, I believe."

"In there," Joe said, pointing to the warehouse where Jellicoe and his henchman had been knocked out.

The officer signaled to his men, and they rushed inside. A moment later Jellicoe emerged, handcuffed and in the company of six officers. He glared at the Hardys as he was shoved into the back of a police car.

Another officer motioned the Hardys to a cruiser and helped them into the backseat. Fire trucks lumbered down the wharf, and the men scrambled to throw intake hoses into the ocean.

In seconds a great plume of water arced over the wharf and descended into the midst of the fire. Already the burning warehouse was little more than a charred wooden skeleton.

Joe couldn't speak. Deep inside he felt a deep rage and a growing refusal to accept the fact that his father had been inside the burning building.

"Jellicoe said something about going to Stockholm," he said to Frank in a calm and collected voice. "He said something about the boss having lots of money stashed there."

Frank nodded. He stared through the window of the police car at the fire fighters battling the flames.

Then he turned away from the blaze to look Joe in the eyes. "Stockholm is a part of all this. It's where Phoenix Enterprises is headquartered."

"So we go to Stockholm," Joe said with an icy calm. "We find the people who killed our father."

"And we bring them to justice," Frank said, turning back to gaze at the hungry flames. "Any way we can."

Next in the Operation Phoenix Trilogy:

For Frank and Joe, a journey in search of justice has turned into a personal mission of revenge. Their intercontinental chase has led them from Kenya to Stockholm, Sweden. Target: Phoenix Enterprises, an international combine of super smugglers that the Hardys hold responsible for their father's death.

But the boys are just beginning to realize how powerful the group is. High-tech weaponry, terrorism, and human suffering are their stock-in-trade. Led on by a beautiful woman, pursued by a trained assassin, the Hardys find danger at every turn. But they'll take any road and any risk to expose the truth—even if it leads across Europe and into the heart of the deadly Phoenix maze . . . in *No Mercy*, Case #65 in The Hardy Boys Casefiles™.